A GIANT
SLICE OF
HORRID
HENRY

D1012913

Francesca Simon spent her childhood on the beach
in California, and then went to Yale and Oxford
Universities to study medieval history and literature.
She now lives in London with her English husband and
their son. When she is not writing books she is doing
theatre and restaurant reviews or chasing after her
Tibetan Spaniel, Shanti.

Also by Francesca Simon

Don't Cook Cinderella
Helping Hercules

There is a complete list of **Horrid Henry** titles
at the end of the book.
Horrid Henry is also available on audio CD and
digital download, all read by Miranda Richardson.

Visit Horrid Henry's website at
www.horridhenry.co.uk for competitions,
games, downloads and a monthly newsletter

A GIANT SLICE OF HORRID HENRY

Francesca Simon
Illustrated by Tony Ross

Orion
Children's Books

First published in Great Britain in 2006
by Orion Children's Books
a division of the Orion Publishing Group Ltd
Orion House
5 Upper St Martin's Lane
London WC2H 9EA

7 9 10 8

ISBN-13 978 1 84255 512 5

A catalogue record for this book is available
from the British Library

Printed in Great Britain by
Clays Ltd, St Ives plc

www.orionbooks.co.uk

CONTENTS

HORRID HENRY'S
STINKBOMB

For Joshua

CONTENTS

1

HORRID HENRY READS A BOOK

Blah blah blah blah blah.

Miss Battle-Axe droned on and on and on. Horrid Henry drew pictures of crocodiles tucking into a juicy Battle-Axe snack in his maths book.

Snap! Off went her head.

Yank! Bye bye leg.

Crunch! Ta-ta teeth.

Yum yum. Henry's crocodile had a big fat smile on its face.

Blah blah blah books blah blah blah read blah blah blah prize blah blah

. . . PRIZE?

Horrid Henry stopped doodling.

"What prize?" he shrieked.

"Don't shout out, Henry," said Miss Battle-Axe.

Horrid Henry waved his hand and shouted:

"What prize?"

"Well, Henry, if you'd been paying attention instead of scribbling, you'd know, wouldn't you?" said Miss Battle-Axe.

Horrid Henry scowled. Typical teacher. You're interested enough in what they're saying to ask a question, and suddenly they don't want to answer.

"So class, as I was saying before I was so rudely interrupted—" she glared at Horrid Henry—"you'll have two weeks to read as many books as you can for our school reading competition. Whoever reads the most books will win an exciting prize. A very exciting prize. But remember, a book report on every book on your list, please."

2

Oh. A reading competition. Horrid Henry slumped in his chair. Phooey. Reading was hard, heavy work. Just turning the pages made Henry feel exhausted. Why couldn't they ever do fun competitions, like whose tummy could rumble the loudest, or who shouted out the most in class, or who knew the rudest words? Horrid Henry would win *those* competitions every time.

But no. Miss Battle-Axe would never have a *fun* competition. Well, no way was he taking part in a reading contest. Henry

would just have to watch someone undeserving like Clever Clare or Brainy Brian swagger off with the prize while he sat prize-less at the back. It was so unfair!

"What's the prize?" shouted Moody Margaret.

Probably something awful like a pencil case, thought Horrid Henry. Or a bumper pack of school tea towels.

"Sweets!" shouted Greedy Graham.

"A million pounds!" shouted Rude Ralph.

"Clothes!" shouted Gorgeous Gurinder.

"A skateboard!" shouted Aerobic Al.

"A hamster!" said Anxious Andrew.

"Silence!" bellowed Miss Battle-Axe. "The prize is a family ticket to a brand new theme park."

Horrid Henry sat up. A theme park! Oh wow! He loved theme parks! Rollercoasters! Water rides! Candy floss!

His mean, horrible parents never took
him to theme parks. They dragged him to
museums. They hauled him on hikes. But
if he won the competition, they'd have to
take him. He had to win that prize. He
had to. But how could he win a reading
competition without reading any books?

"Do comics count?" shouted Rude
Ralph.

Horrid Henry's heart
leapt. He was king of
the comic book readers.
He'd easily win a comic
book competition.

Miss Battle-Axe
glared at Ralph with
her beady eyes.

"Of course not!" she
said. "Clare! How many
books do you think you
can read?"

"Fifteen," said Clever Clare.

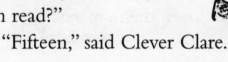

"Brian?"

"Eighteen," said Brainy Brian.

"Nineteen," said Clare.

"Twenty," said Brian.

Horrid Henry smiled. Wouldn't they get a shock when *he* won the prize? He'd start reading the second he got home.

Horrid Henry stretched out in the comfy black chair and switched on the TV. He had plenty of time to read. He'd start tomorrow.

Tuesday. Oh boy! Five new comics!

He'd read them first and start on all those books later.

Wednesday. Whoopee! A Mutant Max TV special! He'd definitely get reading afterwards.

Thursday. Rude Ralph brought round his great new computer game, "Mash 'em! Smash 'em!" Henry mashed and smashed and mashed and smashed . . .

Friday. Yawn. Horrid Henry was exhausted after his long, hard week. I'll read tons of books tomorrow, thought Henry. After all, there was loads of time till the competition ended.

"How many books have *you* read, Henry?" asked Perfect Peter, looking up from the sofa.

"Loads," lied Henry.

"I've read five," said Perfect Peter proudly. "More than anyone in my class."

"Goody for you," said Henry.

7

"You're just jealous," said Peter.

"As if I'd ever be jealous of you, worm," sneered Henry. He wandered over to the sofa. "So what are you reading?"

"*The Happy Nappy*," said Peter.

The Happy Nappy! Trust Peter to read a stupid book like that.

"What's it about?" asked Henry, snorting.

"It's great," said Peter. "It's all about this nappy—" Then he stopped. "Wait, I'm not telling *you*. You just want to find out so you can use it in the competition. Well, you're too late. Tomorrow is the last day."

Horrid Henry felt as if a dagger had been plunged into his heart. This couldn't be. Tomorrow! How had tomorrow sneaked up so fast?

"What!" shrieked Henry. "The competition ends—tomorrow?"

"Yes," said Peter. "You should have

started reading sooner. After all, why put
off till tomorrow what you can do today?"

"Shut up!" said Horrid Henry. He
looked around wildly. What to do, what
to do. He had to read something, anything—fast.

"Gimme that!" snarled Henry, snatching
Peter's book. Frantically, he started to
read:

"I'm unhappy, pappy," said the snappy
nappy. "A happy nappy is a clappy—"

Perfect Peter snatched back his book.

"No!" screamed Peter, holding on
tightly. "It's mine."

Henry lunged.

"Mine!"

"Mine!"

Riii—iippp.

"MUUUUMMMM!" screamed Peter. "Henry tore my book!"

Mum and Dad ran into the room.

"You're fighting—over a book?" said Mum. She sat down in a chair.

"I'm speechless," said Mum.

"Well, I'm not," said Dad. "Henry! Go to your room!"

"Fine!" screamed Horrid Henry.

Horrid Henry prowled up and down his bedroom. He had to think of something. Fast.

Aha! The room was full of books. He'd just copy down lots of titles. Phew. Easy-peasy.

And then suddenly Horrid Henry remembered. He had to write a book

report for every book he read. Rats. Miss
Battle-Axe knew loads and loads of
books. She was sure to know the plot of
Jack the Kangaroo or *The Adventures of Terry
the Tea-Towel*.

Well, he'd just have to borrow Peter's
list.

Horrid Henry sneaked into Peter's
bedroom. There was Peter's competition
entry, in the centre of Peter's immaculate
desk. Henry read it.

Of course Peter would have the
boring and horrible *Mouse Goes to Town*.
Could he live with the shame of having
baby books like *The Happy Nappy* and
Mouse Goes to Town on his competition
entry?

11

For a day at a theme park, anything.

Quickly, Henry copied Peter's list and book reports. Whoopee! Now he had five books. Wheel of Death here I come, thought Horrid Henry.

Then Henry had to face the terrible truth. Peter's books wouldn't be enough to win. He'd heard Clever Clare had seventeen. If only he didn't have to write those book reports. Why oh why did Miss Battle-Axe have to know every book ever written?

And then suddenly Henry had a brilliant, spectacular idea. It was so brilliant, and so simple, that Horrid Henry was amazed. Of course there were books that Miss Battle-Axe didn't know. Books that hadn't been written—yet.

Horrid Henry grabbed his list.

"Mouse Goes to Town. The thrilling adventures of a mouse in town. He meets a dog, a cat, and a duck."

12

Why should that poor mouse just go to town? Quickly Henry began to scribble.

"Mouse Goes to the Country. The thrilling adventures of a mouse in the country. He meets—"

Henry paused. What sort of things *did* you meet in the country? Henry had no idea.

Aha. Henry wrote quickly. "He meets a sheep and a werewolf."

"Mouse Goes Round the World. Mouse discovers that the world is round."

"Mouse Goes to the Loo. The thrilling adventures of one mouse and his potty."

Now, perhaps, something a little different. How about *A Boy and his Pig.* What could that book be about? thought Henry.

"Once upon a time there was a boy and his pig. They played together every day. The pig went oink."

Sounds good to me, thought Henry.

Then there was *A Pig and his Boy.* And, of course, *A Boyish Pig. A Piggish Boy. Two Pigs and a Boy. Two Boys and a Pig.*

Horrid Henry wrote and wrote and wrote. When he had filled up four pages with books and reports, and his hand ached from writing, he stopped and counted.

Twenty-seven books! Surely that was more than enough!

Miss Battle-Axe rose from her seat and walked to the podium in the school hall. Horrid Henry was so excited he could scarcely breathe. He had to win. He was sure to win.

"Well done, everyone," said Miss Battle-Axe. "So many wonderful books read. But sadly, there can be only one winner."

Me! thought Horrid Henry.

"The winner of the school reading competition, the winner who will be receiving a fabulous prize, is—" Horrid Henry got ready to leap up— "Clare, with twenty-eight books!"

Horrid Henry sank back down in his seat as Clever Clare swaggered up to the podium. If only he'd added *Three Boys, Two Pigs, and a Rhinoceros* to his list, he'd have tied for first. It was so unfair. All his hard work for nothing.

"Well done, Clare!" beamed Miss Battle-Axe. She waved Clare's list. "I see you've read one of my very favourites, *Boudicca's Big Battle.*"

She stopped. "Oh dear. Clare, you've put down *Boudicca's Big Battle* twice by mistake. But never mind. I'm sure no one else has read *twenty-seven* books—"

"I have!" screamed Horrid Henry. Leaping and shouting, punching the air with his fist, Horrid Henry ran up onto the stage, chanting: "Theme park! Theme park! Theme park!"

"Gimme my prize!" he screeched, snatching the tickets out of Clare's hand.

16

"Mine!" screamed Clare, snatching them back.

Miss Battle-Axe looked grim. She scanned Henry's list.

"I am not familiar with the *Boy and Pig* series," she said.

"That's 'cause it's Australian," said Horrid Henry.

Miss Battle-Axe glared at him. Then she tried to twist her face into a smile.

"It appears we have a tie," she said. "Therefore, you will each receive a family pass to the new theme park, Book World. Congratulations."

Horrid Henry stopped his victory dance. Book World? Book World? Surely he'd heard wrong?

"Here are just some of the wonderful attractions you will enjoy at Book World," said Miss Battle-Axe. " 'Thrill to a display of speed-reading! Practise checking out library books! Read to the beat!' Oh my, doesn't that sound fun!"

"AAAAAARGGGGGGGGG!" screamed Horrid Henry.

HORRID HENRY'S STINKBOMB

"I hate you, Margaret!" shrieked Sour Susan. She stumbled out of the Secret Club tent.

"I hate you too!" shrieked Moody Margaret.

Sour Susan stuck out her tongue.

Moody Margaret stuck out hers back.

"I quit!" yelled Susan.

"You can't quit. You're fired!" yelled Margaret.

"You can't fire me. I quit!" said Susan.

"I fired you first," said Margaret. "And I'm changing the password!"

"Go ahead. See if I care. I don't want

to be in the Secret Club any more!"
said Susan sourly.

"Good! Because *we* don't want you."

Moody Margaret flounced back inside
the Secret Club tent. Sour Susan stalked
off.

Free at last! Susan was sick and tired of
her ex-best friend Bossyboots Margaret.
Blaming *her* for the disastrous raid on the
Purple Hand Fort when it was all
Margaret's fault was bad enough. But
then to ask stupid Linda to join the
Secret Club without even telling her!
Susan hated Linda even more than she
hated Margaret. Linda hadn't invited
Susan to her sleepover party. And she was
a copycat. But Margaret didn't care. Today
she'd made Linda chief spy. Well, Susan
had had enough. Margaret had been
mean to her once too often.

Susan heard gales of laughter from
inside the club tent. So they were laughing,

were they? Laughing at her, no doubt? Well, she'd show them. She knew all about Margaret's Top Secret Plans. And she knew someone who would be very interested in that information.

"Halt! Password!"

"Smelly toads," said Perfect Peter. He waited outside Henry's Purple Hand Fort.

"Wrong," said Horrid Henry.

"What's the new one then?" said Perfect Peter.

"I'm not telling *you*," said Henry. "You're fired, remember?"

Perfect Peter did remember. He had hoped Henry had forgotten.

"Can't I join again, Henry?" asked Peter.

"No way!" said Horrid Henry.

"Please?" said Perfect Peter.

"No," said Horrid Henry. "Ralph's taken over your duties."

Rude Ralph poked his head through the branches of Henry's lair.

"No babies allowed," said Rude Ralph.

"We don't want you here, Peter," said Horrid Henry. "Get lost."

Perfect Peter burst into tears.

"Crybaby!" jeered Horrid Henry.

"Crybaby!" jeered Rude Ralph.

That did it.

"Mum!" wailed Perfect Peter. He ran towards the house. "Henry won't let me play and he called me a crybaby!"

"Stop being horrid, Henry!" shouted Mum.

Peter waited.

Mum didn't say anything else.

Perfect Peter started to wail louder.

"Muuum! Henry's being mean to me!"

"Leave Peter alone, Henry!" shouted Mum. She came out of the house. Her hands were covered in dough. "Henry, if you don't stop—"

Mum looked around.

"Where's Henry?"

"In his fort," snivelled Peter.

"I thought you said he was being mean to you," said Mum.

"He was!" wailed Peter.

"Just keep away from him," said Mum. She went back into the house.

Perfect Peter was outraged. Was that it? Why hadn't she punished Henry? Henry had been so horrid he deserved to go to prison for a year. Two years. And just get a crust of bread a week. And brussels sprouts. Ha! That would serve Henry right.

25

But until Henry went to prison, how could Peter pay him back?

And then Peter knew exactly what he could do.

He checked carefully to see that no one was watching. Then he sneaked over the garden wall and headed for the Secret Club Tent.

"He isn't!" said Margaret.

"She wouldn't," said Henry.

"He's planning to swap our lemonade for a Dungeon Drink?" said Margaret.

"Yes," said Peter.

"She's planning to stinkbomb the Purple Hand Fort?" said Henry.

"Yes," said Susan.

"How dare she?" said Henry.

"How dare he?" said Margaret. "I'll easily put a stop to that. Linda!" she barked. "Hide the lemonade!"

Linda yawned.

"Hide it yourself," she said. "I'm tired."

Margaret glared at her, then hid the jug under a box.

"Ha ha! Won't Henry be shocked

when he sneaks over and there are no drinks to spike!" gloated Margaret. "Peter, you're a hero. I award you the Triple Star, the highest honour the Secret Club can bestow."

"Ooh, thanks!" said Peter. It was nice being appreciated for a change.

"So from now on," said Moody Margaret, "you're working for me."

"Okay," said the traitor.

Horrid Henry rubbed his hands. This was fantastic! At last, he had a spy in the enemy's camp! He'd easily defend himself against that stupid stinkbomb. Margaret would only let it off when he was *in* the fort. His sentry would be on the lookout armed with a goo-shooter. When

Margaret tried to sneak in with her stinkbomb — ker-pow!

"Hang on a sec," said Horrid Henry, "why should I trust you?"

"Because Margaret is mean and horrible and I hate her," said Susan.

"So from now on," said Horrid Henry, "you're working for me."

Susan wasn't sure she liked the sound of that. Then she remembered Margaret's mean cackle.

"Okay," said the traitor.

Peter sneaked back into his garden and collided with someone.

"Ouch!" said Peter.

"Watch where you're going!" snapped Susan.

They glared at each other suspiciously.

"What were you doing at Margaret's?" said Susan.

"Nothing," said Peter. "What were you doing at my house?"

"Nothing," said Susan.

Peter walked towards Henry's fort, whistling.

Susan walked towards Margaret's tent, whistling.

Well, if Susan was spying on Henry for Margaret, Peter certainly wasn't going to warn him. Serve Henry right.

Well, if Peter was spying on Margaret for Henry, Susan certainly wasn't going to warn her. Serve Margaret right.

Dungeon Drinks, eh?

Margaret liked that idea much better than her stinkbomb plot.

"I've changed my mind about the stinkbomb," said Margaret. "I'm going to swap his drinks for Dungeon Drink stinkers instead."

"Good idea," said Lazy Linda. "Less work."

Stinkbomb, eh?

Henry liked that much better than his dungeon drink plot. Why hadn't he thought of that himself?

"I've changed my mind about the Dungeon Drinks," said Henry. "I'm going to stinkbomb her instead."

"Yeah," said Rude Ralph. "When?"

"Now," said Horrid Henry. "Come on, let's go to my room."

Horrid Henry opened his Stinky Stinkbomb kit. He'd bought it with Grandma. Mum would *never* have let him buy it. But because Grandma had given him the money Mum couldn't do anything about it. Ha ha ha.

Now, which pong would he pick? He looked at the test tubes filled with powder and read the gruesome labels.

Bad breath. Dog poo. Rotten eggs. Smelly socks. Dead fish. Sewer stench.

"I'd go for dead fish," said Ralph. "That's the worst."

Henry considered.

"How about we mix dead fish *and* rotten eggs?"

"Yeah," said Rude Ralph.

Slowly, carefully, Horrid Henry measured out a teaspoon of Dead Fish

powder, and a teaspoon of Rotten Egg
powder, into the special pouch.

Slowly, carefully, Rude Ralph poured
out 150 millilitres of secret stinkbomb
liquid into the bottle and capped it tightly.

All they had to do was to add the powder
to the bottle outside the Secret Club
and—run!

"Ready?" said Horrid Henry.

"Ready," said Rude Ralph.

"Whatever you do," said Horrid
Henry, "don't spill it."

"So you've come crawling back," said
Moody Margaret. "I knew you would."

"No," said Sour Susan. "I just happened to be passing."

She looked around the Secret Club Tent.

"Where's Linda?"

Margaret scowled. "Gone."

"Gone for today, or gone forever?" said Susan.

"Forever," said Margaret savagely. "I don't ever want to see that lazy lump again."

Margaret and Susan looked at each other.

Susan tapped her foot.

Margaret hummed.

"Well?" said Margaret.

"Well what?" said Susan.

"Are you rejoining the Secret Club as Chief Spy or aren't you?"

"I might," said Susan. "And I might not."

"Suit yourself," said Margaret. "I'll call Gurinder and ask her to join instead."

"Okay," said Susan quickly. "I'll join."

Should she mention her visit to
Henry? Better not. After all, what
Margaret didn't know wouldn't hurt her.

"Now, about my stinkbomb plot,"
began Margaret. "I decided—"

Something shattered on the ground
inside the tent. A ghastly, gruesome,
grisly stinky stench filled the air.

"AAAAARGGGGG!" screamed
Margaret, gagging. "It's a —
STINKBOMB!"

"HELP!" shrieked Sour Susan.
"STINKBOMB! Help! Help!"

Victory! Horrid Henry and Rude Ralph ran back to the Purple Hand Fort and rolled round the floor, laughing and shrieking.

What a triumph! Margaret and Susan screaming! Margaret's mum screaming! Margaret's dad screaming! And the stink! Wow! Horrid Henry had never smelled anything so awful in his life.

This called for a celebration.

Horrid Henry offered Ralph a fistful of sweets and poured out two glasses of Fizzywizz drinks.

"Cheers!" said Henry.

"Cheers!" said Ralph.

They drank.

"AAAAAARRGGGGGG!" choked Rude Ralph.

"Bleeeeeech!" yelped Horrid Henry, gagging and spitting. "We've been—" cough!— "Dungeon-Drinked!"

And then Horrid Henry heard a horrible sound. Moody Margaret and Sour Susan were outside the Purple Hand Fort. Chanting a victory chant:

"NAH NAH NE NAH NAH!"

3

HORRID HENRY'S SCHOOL PROJECT

"Susan! Stop shouting!

Ralph! Stop running!

William! Stop weeping!

Henry! Just stop!"

Miss Battle-Axe glared at her class. Her class glared back.

"Miss!" screeched Lazy Linda. "Henry's pulling my hair."

"Miss!" screeched Gorgeous Gurinder. "Ralph's kicking me."

"Miss!" screeched Anxious Andrew. "Dave's poking me."

"Stop it, Henry!" barked Miss Battle-Axe.

Henry stopped. What was bothering the old bat now?

"Class, pay attention," said Miss Battle-Axe. "Today we're doing Group Projects on the Ancient Greeks. We're studying—"

"—the sacking of Troy!" shrieked Henry. Yes! He could see it now. Henry, leading the Greeks as they crashed and slashed their way through the terrified Trojans. His spear would be the longest, and the sharpest, and—

Miss Battle-Axe fixed Henry with her icy stare. Henry froze.

"We're going to divide into small groups and make Parthenons out of cardboard loo rolls and card," continued Miss Battle-Axe. "First you must draw the Parthenon, agree a design together, then build and paint it. I want to see *everyone* sharing and listening. "Also, the Head Teacher will be dropping by to admire your work and to see how beautifully you are working together."

Horrid Henry scowled. He hated working in groups. He detested sharing. He loathed listening to others. Their ideas were always wrong. His ideas were always right. But the other children in Henry's groups never recognised Henry's genius. For some reason they wanted to do things *their* way, not his.

The Ancient Greeks certainly never worked together beautifully, thought Horrid Henry resentfully, so why should he? They just speared each other or ate their children for tea.

"Henry, Bert, William, and Clare, you're working together on Table Three," said Miss Battle-Axe.

Horrid Henry groaned. What a horrible, horrible group. He hated all of them. Why did Miss Battle-Axe never put him in a fun group, with Ralph or Graham or Dave? Henry could see it now. They'd be laughing together in the corner, making trumpets out of loo rolls, sneaking sweets, throwing crayons, flicking paint, having a great time.

But oh no. He had to be with bossy-boots Clare, crybaby William and—Bert. Miss Battle-Axe did it on purpose, just to torture him.

"NO!" protested Horrid Henry. "I can't work with *her*!"

"NO!" protested Clever Clare. "I can't work with *him*!"

"Waaaaah," wailed Weepy William. "I want to work with Andrew."

"Silence!" shouted Miss Battle-Axe. "Now get in your groups and get to work. I want to see everyone sharing and working together beautifully—or else."

There was a mad scramble as everyone ran to their tables to grab the best pencils and the most pieces of paper.

Henry snatched the purple, blue and red pencils and a big pile of paper.

"I haven't got any paper!" screamed William.

"Tough," said Horrid Henry. "I need all these for my design."

"I want some paper!" whined William.

Clever Clare passed him one of her sheets.

William burst into tears.

"It's dirty," he wailed. "And I haven't got a pencil."

"Here's what we're going to do," said Henry. "I'm doing the design, William can help me build it, and everyone can watch me paint."

"No way, Henry," said Clare. "We *all* do a design, then we make the best one."

"Which will be mine," said Horrid Henry.

"Doubt it," said Clever Clare.

"Well I'm not making *yours*," snarled Henry. "And *I'm* doing the painting."

"You're doing the glueing, *I'm* doing the painting," said Clare.

"I want to do the painting," wailed William.

"What do you want to do, Bert?" asked Clare.

"I dunno," said Beefy Bert.

"Fine," said Clever Clare. "Bert will do the tidying. Let's get drawing, everyone. We want our group's Parthenon to be the best."

Horrid Henry was outraged.

"Who made you boss?" demanded Henry.

"Someone has to take charge," said Clever Clare.

Horrid Henry reached under the table and kicked her.

"OOWWWW!" yelped Clever Clare. "Miss! Henry kicked me!"

"Did not!" shouted Horrid Henry. "Liar."

"Why isn't Table Three drawing?"
hissed Miss Battle-Axe.

Clare drew.

William drew.

Bert drew.

Henry drew.

"Everyone should have finished
drawing by now," said Miss Battle-Axe,
patrolling among the tables. "Time to
combine your ideas."

"But I haven't finished," wept William.

Horrid Henry gazed at his design with satisfaction. It was a triumph. He could see it now, painted silver and purple, with a few red stripes.

"Why don't we just build mine?" said Clare.

"'Cos mine's the best!" shouted Horrid Henry.

"What about mine?" whispered William.

"We're building mine!" shouted Clare.

"MINE!"

"MINE!"

Miss Battle-Axe ran over.

"Stop shouting!" shouted Miss Battle-Axe. "Show me your work. That's lovely, Clare. What a fabulous design."

"Thank you, miss," said Clever Clare.

"William! That's a tower, not a temple! Start again!"

"Waaaah!" wailed William.

"Bert! What is this mess?"

"I dunno," said Beefy Bert.

"It looks like a teepee, not a temple," said Miss Battle-Axe.

She looked at Horrid Henry's design and glared at him.

"Can't you follow instructions?" she shrieked. "That temple looks like it's about to blast off."

"That's how I meant it to look," said Henry. "It's high-tech."

48

"Margaret! Sit down! Toby! Leave Brian alone! Graham! Get back to work," said Miss Battle-Axe, racing off to stop the fight on Table Two.

"Right, we're doing *my* design," said Clare. "Who wants to build the steps and who wants to decorate the columns?"

"No one," snapped Horrid Henry, "'cause we're doing *mine*."

"Fine, we'll vote," said Clare. "Who wants to build mine?"

Clare and William raised their hands.

"I'll get you for that, William," muttered Henry.

William burst into tears.

"Who wants to do Henry's?" said Clare.

Only Henry raised his hand.

"Come on Bert, don't you want to make mine?" pleaded Henry.

"I dunno," said Beefy Bert.

"It's not fair!" shrieked Horrid Henry. "I WANT TO BUILD MINE!"

49

"MINE!"

"MINE!"

"SLAP!"

"SLAP!

"That's it!" shrieked Miss Battle-Axe. "Henry! Work in the corner on your own."

YES! This was the best news Henry had heard all morning.

Beaming, Henry went to the corner and sat down at his own little table, with his own glue, his own scissors, his own paints, his own card, and his own pile of loo rolls.

Bliss, thought Henry. I can build my Parthenon in peace.

There was just one problem. There was only a small number of loo rolls left.

This isn't nearly enough for my Parthenon, thought Horrid Henry. I need more.

He went over to Moody Margaret's table.

"I need more loo rolls," he said.

"Tough," said Margaret, "we're using all of ours."

Henry stomped over to Sour Susan's table.

"Give me some loo rolls," he said.

"Go away," said Susan sourly. "Margaret took our extras."

"Sit down, Henry," barked Miss Battle-Axe.

Henry sat, fuming. This was an outrage. Hadn't Miss Battle-Axe told them to

share? And here were his greedy class-
mates hogging all the loo rolls when his
Parthenon desperately needed extra
engines.

BUZZZ. Breaktime!

"Leave your Parthenons on the tables
to dry," said Miss Battle-Axe. "Henry, you
will stay in at break and finish."

What?

Miss break?

"But—but—"

"Sit down," ordered Miss Battle-Axe.
"Or you'll go straight to the Head!"

Eeeek! Horrid Henry knew the Head,
Mrs Oddbod, all too well. He did not
need to know her any better.

Henry slunk back to his chair.
Everyone else ran shrieking out of the
door to the playground. Why was it
always children who were punished? Why
weren't teachers ever sent to the Head? It
was so unfair!

"I just have to nip down the hall for a moment. Don't you dare leave that table," said Miss Battle-Axe.

The moment Miss Battle-Axe left the room, Henry jumped up and accidentally on purpose knocked over Clare's chair. He broke William's pencil and drew a skull and crossbones on Bert's teepee.

Then he wandered over to Sour Susan's table. There was a freshly-glued Parthenon, waiting to be painted.

Henry studied it.

You know, he thought, Susan's group hasn't done a bad job. Not bad at all. Shame about that bulge on the side, though. If they shared one loo roll with me, it would balance so much better.

Horrid Henry looked to the left.

He looked to the right.

Snatch! Susan's supports sagged.

Better even that up, thought Horrid Henry.

Yank!

Hmmn, thought Horrid Henry, glancing at Gurinder's table. What were they thinking? Those walls are far too tall.

Grab! Gurinder's temple tottered.

And as for Clare's pathetic efforts, it was positively bursting with useless pillars.

Whisk! Clare's columns wobbled.

Much better, thought Horrid Henry. Soon he had plenty of loo rolls.

CLOMP

CLOMP

CLOMP

Horrid Henry dashed back to his table and was

innocently glueing away as the class stampeded back to their tables.

Wobble

Wobble

Wobble—CRASH!

On every table, Parthenons started collapsing.

Everyone shrieked and screamed and sobbed.

"It's your fault!"

"Yours!"

"You didn't glue it right!"

"You didn't build it right!"

Rude Ralph hurled a paintbrush at Moody Margaret. Margaret hurled it back. Suddenly the room was filled with flying brushes, gluepots and loo rolls.

Miss Battle-Axe burst in.

"STOP IT!" bellowed Miss Battle-Axe, as a loo roll hit her on the nose. "YOU ARE THE WORST CLASS I HAVE EVER TAUGHT! I LEAVE YOU ALONE FOR ONE MINUTE AND JUST LOOK AT THIS MESS! NOW SIT DOWN AND SHUT—"

The door opened. In walked the Head.

Mrs Oddbod stared at Miss Battle-Axe.

Miss Battle-Axe stared at Mrs Oddbod.

"Boudicca!" said Mrs Oddbod. "What-is-going-on?"

"The sacking of Troy!" shrieked Horrid Henry.

There was a terrible silence.

Horrid Henry shrank in his seat. Now he was done for. Now he was dead.

"I can see that," said Mrs Oddbod

58

coldly. "Miss Battle-Axe! Come to my office—now!"

"No!" whimpered Miss Battle-Axe.

YES! thought Horrid Henry.

Victory!

4

HORRID HENRY'S SLEEPOVER

Horrid Henry loved sleepovers. Midnight feasts! Pillow fights! Screaming and shouting! Rampaging till dawn!

The time he ate all the ice cream at Greedy Graham's and left the freezer door open! The time he jumped on all the beds at Dizzy Dave's and broke them all. And that time at Rude Ralph's when he—well, hmmn, perhaps better not mention that.

There was just one problem. No one would ever have Horrid Henry at their house for a sleepover more than once. Whenever Henry went to sleep at a friend's house, Mum and Dad were sure

to get a call at three a.m.
from a demented parent
screaming at them to
pick up Henry imme-
diately.

Horrid Henry
couldn't understand it.
Parents were so fussy.
Even the parents of great
kids like Rude Ralph and
Greedy Graham. Who cares about a little
noise? Or a broken bed? Big deal,
thought Horrid Henry.

It was no fun having friends sleep over
at *his* house. There was no rampaging and
feasting at Henry's. It was lights out as
usual at nine o'clock, no talking, no
feasting, no fun.

So when New Nick, who had just
joined Henry's class, invited Henry to
stay the night, Horrid Henry couldn't
believe his luck. New beds to bounce on.

New biscuit tins to raid. New places to rampage. Bliss!

Henry packed his sleepover bag as fast as he could.

Mum came in. She looked grumpy.

"Got your pyjamas?" she asked.

Henry never needed pyjamas at sleepovers because he never went to bed.

"Got them," said Henry. Just not *with* him, he thought.

"Don't forget your toothbrush," said Mum.

"I won't," said Horrid Henry. He never *forgot* his toothbrush—he just chose not to bring it.

Dad came in. He looked even grumpier.

"Don't forget your comb," said Dad.

Horrid Henry looked at his bulging backpack stuffed with toys and comics. Sadly, there was no room for a comb.

"I won't," lied Henry.

"I'm warning you, Henry," said Mum. "I want you to be on best behaviour tonight."

"Of course," said Horrid Henry.

"I don't want any phone calls at three a.m. from Nick's parents," said Dad. "If I do, this will be your last sleepover ever. I mean it."

Nag nag nag.

"All right," said Horrid Henry.

Ding Dong.

WOOF WOOF WOOF WOOF WOOF!

A woman opened the door. She was wearing a Viking helmet on her head and long flowing robes. Behind her stood a man in a velvet cloak holding back five enormous, snarling black dogs.

"TRA LA LA BOOM-DY AY," boomed a dreadful, ear-splitting voice.

"Bravo, Bravo!" shouted a chorus from the sitting room.

GRRRRRRR! growled the dogs.

Horrid Henry hesitated. Did he have the right house? Was New Nick an alien?

"Oh don't mind us, dear, it's our opera club's karaoke night," trilled the Viking helmet.

"Nick!" bellowed the Cloak. "Your friend is here."

Nick appeared. Henry was glad to see he was not wearing a Viking helmet or a velvet cloak.

"Hi Henry," said New Nick.

"Hi Nick," said Horrid Henry.

A little girl toddled over, sucking her thumb.

"Henry, this is my sister, Lily," said Nick.

Lily gazed at Horrid Henry.

"I love you, Henwy," said Lisping Lily.

"Will you marry with me?"

"NO!" said Horrid Henry. Uggh.
What a revolting thought.

"Go away, Lily," said Nick.

Lily did not move.

"Come on, Nick, let's get out of here,"
said Henry. No toddler was going to spoil
his fun. Now, what would he do first, raid
the kitchen, or bounce on the beds?

"Let's raid the kitchen," said Henry.

"Great," said Nick.

"Got any good sweets?" asked Henry.

"Loads!" said New Nick.

Yeah! thought Horrid Henry. His sleepover fun was beginning!

They sneaked into the kitchen. The floor was covered with dog blankets, overturned food bowls, clumps of dog hair, and gnawed dog bones. There were a few suspicious looking puddles. Henry hoped they were water.

"Here are the biscuits," said Nick.

Henry looked. Were those dog hairs all over the jar?

"Uh, no thanks," said Henry. "How about some sweets?"

"Sure," said Nick. "Help yourself."

He handed Henry a bar of chocolate. Yummy! Henry was about to take a big

bite when he stopped. Were those—teeth
marks in the corner?

"RAAA!" A big black shape jumped
on Henry, knocked him down, and
snatched the chocolate.

Nick's dad burst in.

"Rigoletto! Give that back!" said
Nick's dad, yanking the chocolate out of
the dog's mouth.

"Sorry about that, Henry," he said,
offering it back to Henry.

"Uhh, maybe later," said Henry.

"Okay," said Nick's dad, putting
the slobbery chocolate back in the
cupboard.

Eeew, gross, thought Horrid Henry.

"I love you, Henwy," came a lisping
voice behind him.

"AH HA HA HA HA HA HA HA!"
warbled a high, piercing voice from the
sitting room.

Henry held his ears. Would the
windows shatter?

"Encore!" shrieked the opera karaoke
club.

"Will you marry with me?" asked
Lisping Lily.

70

"Let's get out of here," said Horrid Henry.

Horrid Henry leapt on Nick's bed.

Yippee, thought Horrid Henry. Time to get bouncing.

Bounce–

Crash!

The bed collapsed in a heap.

"What happened?" said Henry. "I hardly did anything."

"Oh, I broke the bed ages ago," said Nick. "Dad said he was tired of fixing it."

Rats, thought Henry. What a lazy dad.

"How about a pillow fight?" said Henry.

"No pillows," said Nick. "The dogs chewed them."

Hmmn.

They *could* sneak down and raid the freezer, but for some reason Henry didn't really want to go back into that kitchen.

"I know!" said Henry. "Let's watch TV."

"Sure," said New Nick.

"Where is the TV?" said Henry.

"In the sitting room," said Nick.

"But—the karaoke," said Henry.

"Oh, they won't mind," said Nick. "They're used to noise in this house."

"DUM DUM DE DUM DUMM DUMM

DUM DE DUM DUMM DUMM–"

Horrid Henry sat with his face pressed to the TV. He couldn't hear a word Mutant Max was shrieking with all that racket in the background.

"Maybe we should go to bed," said Horrid Henry, sighing. Anything to get away from the noise.

"Okay," said New Nick.

Phew, thought Horrid Henry. Peace at last.

SNORE! SNORE!

Horrid Henry turned over in his
sleeping bag and tried to get comfortable.
He hated sleeping on the floor. He hated
sleeping with the window open. He
hated sleeping with the radio on. And he
hated sleeping in the same room with

73

someone who snored.

Awhooooooo! howled the winter wind through the open window.

SNORE! SNORE!

"I'm just a lonesome cowboy, lookin' for a lonesome cowgirl," blared the radio.

WOOF WOOF WOOF barked the dogs.

"Yeowwww!" squealed Henry, as five

wet, smelly dogs pounced on him.

"Awhoooo!" howled the wind.

SNORE! SNORE!

"TOREADOR—on guard!" boomed the opera karaoke downstairs.

Horrid Henry loved noise. But this was—too much.

He'd have to find somewhere else to sleep.

Horrid Henry flung open the bedroom door.

"I love you Henwy," said Lisping Lily.

Slam! Horrid Henry shut the bedroom door.

Horrid Henry did not move.

Horrid Henry did not breathe.

Then he opened the door a fraction.

"Will you marry with me, Henwy?"

Aaarrrgh!!!

Horrid Henry ran from the bedroom and barricaded himself in the linen cupboard. He settled down on a pile of towels.

Phew. Safe at last.

"I want to give you a big kiss, Henwy," came a little voice beside him.

NOOOOOOOO!

It was three a.m.

"TRA LA LA BOOM-DY AY!"

"—LONESOME COWBOY!"

SNORE! SNORE!

AWHOOOOOOOOOOOOOO!

WOOF! WOOF! WOOF!

Horrid Henry crept to the hall phone and dialled his number.

Dad answered.

"I'm so sorry about Henry, do you want us to come and get him?" Dad mumbled.

"Yes," wailed Horrid Henry. "I need my rest!"

HORRID
HENRY'S
UNDERPANTS

For Gina Kovarsky

CONTENTS

1

HORRID HENRY EATS A VEGETABLE

"Ugggh! Gross! Yuck! Bleeeeeech!"

Horrid Henry glared at the horrible, disgusting food slithering on his plate. Globby slobby blobs. Bumpy lumps. Rubbery blubbery globules of glop. Ugghh!

How Dad and Mum and Peter could eat this swill without throwing up was amazing. Henry poked at the white, knobbly clump. It looked like brains. It felt like brains. Maybe it was . . . Ewwwwwwww.

Horrid Henry pushed away his plate.

"I can't eat this," moaned Henry. "I'll be sick!"

"Henry! Cauliflower cheese is delicious," said Mum.

"And nutritious," said Dad.

"I love it," said Perfect Peter. "Can I have seconds?"

"It's nice to know *someone* appreciates my cooking," said Dad. He frowned at Henry.

"But I hate vegetables," said Henry. Yuck. Vegetables were so . . . healthy. And tasted so . . . vegetably. "I want pizza!"

"Well, you can't have it," said Dad.

"Ralph has pizza and chips every night at *his* house," said Henry. "And Graham *never* has to eat vegetables."

"I don't care what Ralph and Graham eat," said Mum.

"You've got to eat more vegetables," said Dad.

"I eat loads of vegetables," said Henry.

"Name one," said Dad.

"Crisps," said Henry.

"Crisps aren't vegetables, are they, Mum?" said Perfect Peter.

"No," said Mum. "Go on, Henry."

"Ketchup," said Henry.

"Ketchup is not a vegetable," said Dad.

"It's impossible cooking for you," said Mum.

"You're such a picky eater," said Dad.

"I eat loads of things," said Henry.

"Like what?" said Dad.

"Chips. Crisps. Burgers. Pizza. Chocolate. Sweets. Cake. Biscuits. Loads of food," said Horrid Henry.

"That's not very healthy, Henry," said Perfect Peter. "You haven't said any fruit or vegetables."

"So?" said Henry. "Mind your own business, Toad."

"Henry called me Toad," wailed Peter.

"Ribbet. Ribbet," croaked Horrid Henry.

"Don't be horrid, Henry," snapped Dad.

"You can't go on eating so unhealthily," said Mum.

"Agreed," said Dad.

Uh oh, thought Henry. Here it comes. Nag nag nag. If there were prizes for best naggers Mum and Dad would win every time.

"I'll make a deal with you, Henry," said Mum.

"What?" said Henry suspiciously. Mum and Dad's "deals" usually involved his doing something horrible, for a pathetic

reward. Well no way was he falling for
that again.

"If you eat all your vegetables for five
nights in a row, we'll take you to Gobble
and Go."

Henry's heart missed a beat. Gobble
and Go! Gobble and Go! Only Henry's
favourite restaurant in the whole wide
world. Their motto: "The chips just keep
on coming!" shone forth from a purple
neon sign. Music blared from twenty
loudspeakers. Each table had its own TV.
You could watch the chefs heat up your
food in a giant microwave. Best of all,
grown-ups never wanted to hang about
for hours and chat. You ordered, gobbled,
and left. Heaven.

And what fantastic food! Jumbo
burgers. Huge pizzas. Lakes of ketchup. As
many chips as you could eat. Fifty-two
different ice creams. And not a vegetable
in sight.

For some reason Mum and Dad hated Gobble and Go. They'd taken him once, and sworn they would never go again.

And now, unbelievably, Mum was offering.

"Deal!" shouted Henry, in case she changed her mind.

"So we're agreed," said Mum. "You eat your vegetables every night for five nights, and then we'll go."

"Sure. Whatever," said Horrid Henry eagerly. He'd agree to anything for a meal at Gobble and Go. He'd agree to dance naked down the street singing "Hallelujah! I'm a nudie!" for the chance to eat at Gobble and Go.

Perfect Peter stopped eating his cauliflower. He didn't look very happy.

"I always eat *my* vegetables," said Peter. "What's my reward?"

"Health," said Mum.

Day 1. String beans.

"Mum, Henry hasn't eaten any beans yet," said Peter.

"I have too," lied Henry.

"No you haven't," said Peter. "I've been watching."

"Shut up, Peter," said Henry.

"Mum!" wailed Peter. "Henry told me to shut up."

"Don't tell your brother to shut up," said Mum.

"It's rude," said Dad. "Now eat your veg."

Horrid Henry glared at his plate, teeming with slimy string beans. Just like a bunch of green worms, he thought. Yuck.

He must have been
mad agreeing to eat
vegetables for five
nights in a row.
He'd be poisoned
before day three.
Then they'd be sorry.
"How could we have been so
cruel?" Mum would shriek. "We've killed
our own son," Dad would moan. "Why
oh why did we make him eat his
greens?" they would sob.

Too bad he'd be dead so he couldn't
scream, "I told you so!"

"We have a deal, Henry," said Dad.

"I know," snapped Henry.

He cut off the teeniest, tiniest bit of
string bean he could.

"Go on," said Mum.

Slowly, Horrid Henry lifted his fork
and put the poison in his mouth.

Aaaarrrgggghhhhhh! What a horrible

taste! Henry spat and spluttered as the sickening sliver of string bean stuck in his throat.

"Water!" he gasped.

Perfect Peter speared several beans and popped them in his mouth.

"Great string beans, Dad," said Peter. "So crispy and crunchy."

"Have mine if you like them so much," muttered Henry.

"I want to see you eat every one of those string beans," said Dad. "Or no Gobble and Go."

Horrid Henry scowled. No way was he eating another mouthful. The taste was too horrible. But, oh, Gobble and Go. Those burgers! Those chips! Those TVs!

There had to be another way. Surely he, King Henry the Horrible, could defeat a plate of greens?

Horrid Henry worked out his battle

plan. It was dangerous. It was risky. But what choice did he have?

First, he had to distract the enemy.

"You know, Mum," said Henry, pretending to chew, "you were right. These beans *are* very tasty."

Mum beamed.

Dad beamed.

"I told you you'd like them if you tried them," said Mum.

Henry pretended to swallow, then speared another bean. He pushed it round his plate.

Mum got up to refill the water jug. Dad turned to speak to her. Now was his chance!

Horrid Henry stretched out his foot
under the table and lightly tickled Peter's
leg.

"Look out, Peter, there's a spider on
your leg."

"Where?" squealed Peter, looking
frantically under the table.

Leap! Plop!

Henry's beans hopped onto Peter's
plate.

Peter raised his head.

"I don't see any spider," said Peter.

"I knocked it off," mumbled Henry, pretending to chew vigorously.

Then Peter saw his plate, piled high with string beans.

"Ooh," said Peter, "lucky me! I thought I'd finished!"

Tee hee, thought Horrid Henry.

Day 2. Broccoli.

Plip!

A piece of Henry's broccoli "accidentally" fell on the floor. Henry kicked it under Peter's chair.

Plop! Another piece of Henry's broccoli fell. And another. And another.

Plip plop. Plip plop. Plip plop.

Soon the floor under Peter's chair was littered with broccoli bits.

"Mum!" said Henry. "Peter's making a mess."

"Don't be a telltale, Henry," said Dad.

"He's always telling on *me*," said
Henry.

Dad checked under Peter's chair.

"Peter! Eat more carefully. You're not a
baby any more."

Ha ha ha thought Horrid Henry.

Day 3. Peas.

Squish!

Henry flattened a pea under his knife.

Squash!

Henry flattened another one.

Squish. Squash.

Squish. Squash.

Soon every
pea was safely
squished and
hidden under Henry's knife.

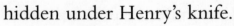

"Great dinner, Dad," said Horrid
Henry. "Especially the peas. I'll clear," he
added, carrying his plate to the sink and
quickly rinsing his knife.

Dad beamed.

"Eating vegetables is making you helpful," said Dad.

"Yes," said Henry sweetly. "It's great being helpful."

Day 4. Cabbage.

Buzz.

Buzz.

"A fly landed on my cabbage!" shrieked Henry. He swatted the air with his hands.

"Where?" said Mum.

"There!" said Henry. He leapt out of his seat. "Now it's on the fridge!"

"Buzz," said Henry under his breath.

"I don't see any fly," said Dad.

"Up there!" said Henry, pointing to the ceiling.

Mum looked up.

Dad looked up.

Peter looked up.

Henry dumped a handful of cabbage in the bin. Then he sat back down at the table.

"Rats," said Henry. "I can't eat the rest of my cabbage now, can I? Not after a filthy horrible disgusting fly has walked all over it, spreading germs and dirt and poo and—"

"All right all right," said Dad. "Leave the rest."

I am a genius, thought Horrid Henry, smirking. Only one more battle until – Vegetable Victory!

Day 5. Sprouts.

Mum ate her sprouts.

Dad ate his sprouts.

Peter ate his sprouts.

Henry glared at his sprouts. Of all the miserable, rotten vegetables ever invented, sprouts were the worst. So bitter. So stomach-churning. So . . . green.

But how to get rid of them? There was Peter's head, a tempting target. A very tempting target. Henry's sprout-flicking fingers itched. No, thought Horrid Henry. I can't blow it when I'm so close.

Should he throw them on the floor? Spit them in his napkin?

Or – Horrid Henry beamed.

There was a little drawer in the table in front of Henry's chair. A perfect, brussels sprout-sized drawer.

Henry eased it open. What could be simpler than stuffing a sprout or two inside while pretending to eat?

Soon the drawer was full. Henry's plate was empty.

"Look Mum! Look Dad!" screeched Henry. "All gone!" Which was true, he thought gleefully.

"Well done, Henry," said Dad.

"Well done, Henry," said Peter.

"We'll take you to Gobble and Go tomorrow," said Mum.

"Yippee!" screamed Horrid Henry.

Mum, Dad, Henry, and Peter walked up the street.

Mum, Dad, Henry, and Peter walked down the street.

Where was Gobble and Go, with its flashing neon sign, blaring music, and purple walls? They must have walked past it.

But how? Horrid Henry looked about wildly. It was impossible to miss Gobble and Go. You could see that neon sign for miles.

"It was right here," said Horrid Henry.

But Gobble and Go was gone.

A new restaurant squatted in its place.

"The Virtuous Veggie," read the sign. "The all new, vegetable restaurant!"

Horrid Henry gazed in horror at the menu posted outside.

Cabbage Casserole
Pop-up Peas
Spinach Surprise
Sprouts a go-go
Choice of rhubarb or broccoli ice cream

"Yummy!" said Perfect Peter.

"Look, Henry," said Mum. "It's serving all your new favourite vegetables."

Horrid Henry opened his mouth to protest. Then he closed it. He knew when he was beaten.

2

HORRID HENRY'S UNDERPANTS

A late birthday present! Whoopee! Just when you thought you'd got all your loot, more treasure arrives.

Horrid Henry shook the small thin package. It was light. Very light. Maybe it was — oh, please let it be — MONEY! Of course it was money. What else could it be? There was so much stuff he needed: a Mutant Max lunchbox, a Rapper Zapper Blaster, and, of course, the new Terminator Gladiator game he kept seeing advertised on TV. Mum and Dad were so mean and horrible, they wouldn't buy it for him. But he could buy whatever he liked with his own

money. So there. Ha ha ha ha ha.
Wouldn't Ralph be green with envy
when he swaggered into school with a
Mutant Max lunchbox? And no way
would he even let Peter touch his
Rapper Zapper Blaster.

So how much money had he been
sent? Maybe enough for him to buy
everything! Horrid Henry tore off the
wrapping paper.

AAAAARRRRGGGHHHHH!
Great-Aunt Greta had done it again.

Great-Aunt Greta thought he was a
girl. Great-Aunt Greta had been told ten
billion times that his name was Henry,
not Henrietta, and that he wasn't four
years old. But every year Peter would get
£10, or a football, or a computer game,
and Henry would get a Walkie-Talkie-
Teasy-Weasy-Burpy-Slurpy Doll. Or a
Princess Pamper Parlour. Or Baby Poopie
Pants. And now this.

Horrid Henry picked up the birthday card. Maybe there was money inside. He opened it.

Dear Henny,
You must be such a big girl now, so I know you'd love a pair of big girl pants. I'll bet pink is your favourite colour.
Love, Great-Aunt Greta

Horrid Henry stared in horror at the frilly pink lacy knickers, decorated with glittery hearts and bows. This was the worst present he had ever received. Worse than socks. Worse than handkerchiefs. Even worse than a book.

Bleeech! Ick! Yuck! Horrid Henry chucked the hideous underpants in the bin where they belonged.

Ding dong.

Oh no! Rude Ralph was here to play.
If he saw those knickers Henry would
never hear the end of it. His name would
be mud forever.

Clump clump clump.

Ralph was stomping up the stairs to his
bedroom. Henry snatched the terrible pants
from the bin and looked around his room
wildly for a hiding place. Under the pillow?
What if they had a pillow fight? Under the
bed? What if they played hide and seek?
Quickly Henry stuffed them in the back of
his pants drawer. I'll get rid of them the
moment Ralph leaves, he thought.

"Mercy, Your
Majesty, mercy!"
King Henry the
Horrible looked
down at his
snivelling brother.

"Off with his head!" he ordered.

"Henry! Henry! Henry!" cheered his grateful subjects.

"HENRY!"

King Henry the Horrible woke up. His Medusa mother was looming above him.

"You've overslept!" shrieked Mum. "School starts in five minutes! Get dressed! Quick! Quick!" She pulled the duvet off Henry.

"Wha—wha?" mumbled Henry.

Dad raced into the room.

"Hurry!" shouted Dad. "We're late!" He yanked Henry out of bed.

Henry stumbled around his dark bedroom. Half-asleep, he reached inside his underwear drawer, grabbed a pair, then picked up some clothes off the floor and flung everything on. Then he, Dad, and Peter ran all the way to school.

"Margaret! Stop pulling Susan's hair!"

"Ralph! Sit down!"

"Linda! Sit up!"

"Henry! Pay attention!" barked Miss Battle-Axe. "I am about to explain long division. I will only explain it once. You take a great big number, like 374, and then divide it—"

Horrid Henry was not paying attention. He was tired. He was crabby. And for some reason his pants were itchy.

These pants feel horrible, he thought. And so tight. What's wrong with them?

Horrid Henry sneaked a peek.

And then Horrid Henry saw what

pants he had on. Not
his Driller Cannibal
pants. Not his
Marvin the Maniac
ones either. Not
even his old Gross-
Out ones, with the
holes and the droopy
elastic.

He, Horrid Henry, was wearing frilly
pink lacy girls' pants covered in glittery
hearts and bows. He'd completely forgotten
he'd stuffed them into his pants drawer last
month so Ralph wouldn't see them. And
now, oh horror of horrors, he was wearing
them.

Maybe it's a nightmare, thought
Horrid Henry hopefully. He pinched his
arm. Ouch! Then, just to be sure, he
pinched William.

"Waaaaah!" wailed Weepy William.

"Stop weeping, William!" said Miss

Battle-Axe. "Now, what number do I need—"

It was not a nightmare. He was still in school, still wearing pink pants.

What to do, what to do?

Don't panic, thought Horrid Henry. He took a deep breath. Don't panic. After all, no one will know. His trousers weren't see-through or anything.

Wait. What trousers was he wearing? Were there any holes in them? Quickly Horrid Henry twisted round to check his bottom.

Phew. There were no holes. What luck he hadn't put on his old jeans with the big rip but a new pair.

He was safe.

"Henry! What's the answer?" said Miss Battle-Axe.

"Pants," said Horrid Henry before he could stop himself.

The class burst out laughing.

"Pants!" screeched Rude Ralph.

"Pants!" screeched Dizzy Dave.

"Henry. Stand up," ordered Miss Battle-Axe.

Henry stood. His heart was pounding. Slip!

Aaaarrrghhh! The lacy ruffle of his pink pants was showing! His new trousers were too big. Mum always bought him clothes that were way too big so he'd grow into them. These were the falling-down ones he'd tried on yesterday. Henry gripped his trousers tight and yanked them up.

"What did you say?" said Miss Battle-Axe slowly.

"Ants," said Horrid Henry.

"Ants?" said Miss Battle-Axe.

"Yeah," said Henry quickly. "I was just thinking about how many ants you could divide by — by that number you said," he added.

Miss Battle-Axe glared at him.

"I've got my eye on you, Henry," she snapped. "Now sit down and pay attention."

Henry sat. All he had to do was tuck in his T-shirt. That would keep his trousers up. He'd look stupid but for once Henry didn't care.

Just so long as no one ever knew about his pink lacy pants.

And then Henry's blood turned to ice. What was the latest craze on the playground? De-bagging. Who'd started it? Horrid Henry. Yesterday he'd chased Dizzy

114

Dave and pulled down his trousers. The day before he'd done the same thing to Rude Ralph. Just this morning he'd de-bagged Tough Toby on the way into class.

They'd all be trying to de-bag him now.

I have to get another pair of pants, thought Henry desperately.

Miss Battle-Axe passed round the maths worksheets. Quickly Horrid Henry scribbled down: 3, 7, 41, 174, without reading any questions. He didn't have time for long division.

Where could he find some other pants?
He could pretend to be sick and get sent
home from school. But he'd already tried
that twice this week. Wait. Wait. He was
brilliant. He was a genius. What about the
Lost and Found? Someone, some time,
must have lost some pants.

DING! DING!

Before the playtime bell had finished
ringing Horrid Henry was out of his
seat and racing down the hall, holding
tight to his trousers. He checked carefully
to make sure no one was watching,
then ducked into the Lost and Found.
He'd hide here until he found some
pants.

The Lost and Found was stuffed with
clothes. He rummaged through the
mountains of lost shoes, socks, jackets,
trousers, shirts, coats, lunchboxes, hats,
and gloves. I'm amazed anyone leaves
school wearing *anything*, thought Horrid

Henry, tossing another sweatshirt over his
shoulder.

Then – hurray! Pants. A pair of blue
pants. What a wonderful sight.

Horrid Henry pulled the pants from
the pile. Oh no. They were the teeniest,
tiniest pair he'd ever seen. Some toddler
must have lost them.

Rats, thought Horrid Henry. Well,
no way was he wearing his horrible
pink pants a second longer. He'd just
have to trade pants with someone.
And Horrid Henry had the perfect
someone in mind.

Henry found Peter in the playground playing tag with Tidy Ted.

"I need to talk to you in private," said Henry. "It's urgent."

"What about?" said Peter cautiously.

"It's top secret," said Henry. Out of the corner of his eye he saw Dave and Toby sneaking towards him.

Top secret! Henry never shared top secret secrets with Peter.

"Quick!" yelped Henry. "There's no time to lose!"

He ducked into the boys' toilet. Peter followed.

"Peter, I'm worried about you," said Horrid Henry. He tried to look concerned.

"I'm fine," said Peter.

"No you're not," said Henry. "I've heard bad things about you."

"What bad things?" said Peter anxiously. Not — not that he had run across the carpet in class?

"Embarrassing rumours," said Horrid
Henry. "But if I don't tell you, who will?
After all," he said, putting his arm around
Peter's shoulder, "it's my job to look after
you. Big brothers should look out for
little ones."

Perfect Peter could not believe his
ears.

"Oh, Henry," said Peter. "I've always
wanted a brother who looked after me."

"That's me," said Henry. "Now listen.
I've heard you wear baby pants."

"I do not," said Peter. "Look!" And he

showed Henry his Daffy and her Dancing Daisies pants.

Horrid Henry's heart went cold. Daffy and her Dancing Daisies! Ugh. Yuck. Gross. But even Daffy would be a million billion times better than pink pants with lace ruffles.

"Daffy Daisy are the most babyish pants you could wear," said Henry. "Worse than wearing a nappy. Everyone will tease you."

Peter's lip trembled. He hated being teased.

"What can I do?" he asked.

Henry pretended to think. "Look. I'll do you a big favour. I'll swap my pants for yours. That way *I'll* get teased, not you."

"Thank you, Henry," said Peter. "You're the best brother in the world." Then he stopped.

"Wait a minute," he said suspiciously, "let's see your pants."

"Why?" said Henry.

"Because," said Peter, "how do I know you've even got pants to swap?"

Horrid Henry was outraged.

"Of course I've got pants," said Henry.

"Then show me," said Peter.

Horrid Henry was trapped.

"OK," he said, giving Peter a quick flash of pink lace.

Perfect Peter stared at Henry's underpants.

"Those are your pants?" he said.

"Sure," said Horrid Henry. "These are big boy pants."

"But they're pink," said Peter.

"All big boys wear pink," said Henry.

"But they have lace on them," said Peter.

"All big boys' pants have lace," said Henry.

"But they have hearts and bows," said Peter.

"Of course they do, they're big boy pants," said Horrid Henry. "You wouldn't know because you only wear baby pants."

Peter hesitated.

"But . . . but . . . they look like — girls' pants," said Peter.

Henry snorted. "Girls' pants! Do you think *I'd* ever wear girls' pants? These are what all the big kids are wearing. You'll be the coolest kid in class in these."

Perfect Peter backed away.

"No I won't," said Peter.

"Yes you will," said Henry.

"I don't want to wear your smelly pants," said Peter.

"They're not smelly," said Henry. "They're brand new. Now give me your pants."

"NO!" screamed Peter.

"YES!" screamed Henry. "Give me your pants!"

"What's going on in here?" came a voice of steel. It was the Head, Mrs Oddbod.

"Nothing," said Henry.

"There's no hanging about the toilets at playtime," said Mrs Oddbod. "Out of here, both of you."

Peter ran out the door.

Now what do I do, thought Horrid Henry.

Henry ducked into a stall and hid the pink pants on the ledge above the third toilet. No way was he putting those pants back on. Better Henry no pants than Henry pink pants.

★

At lunchtime Horrid Henry dodged
Graham. He dodged Toby by the
climbing frame. During last play Dave
almost caught him by the water
fountain but Henry was too quick.
Ralph chased him into class but Henry
got to his seat just in time. He'd done
it! Only forty-five minutes to go until
home time. There'd be no de-bagging
after school with parents around.
Henry couldn't believe it. He was safe
at last.

He stuck out his tongue at Ralph.

"Nah nah ne nah ne," he jeered.

Miss Battle-Axe clapped her claws.

"Time to change for P.E," said Miss
Battle-Axe.

P.E! It couldn't be – not a P.E. day.

"And I don't care if aliens stole your
P.E. kit, Henry," said Miss Battle-Axe,
glaring at him. "No excuses."

That's what she thought. He had the

perfect excuse. Even a teacher as mean
and horrible as Miss Battle-Axe would
not force a boy to do P.E. without pants.

Horrid Henry went up to Miss Battle-
Axe and whispered in her ear.

"Forgot your pants, eh?" barked
Miss Battle-Axe loudly.

Henry blushed
scarlet. When
he was king
he'd make
Miss Battle-
Axe walk
around town every
day wearing pants on her head.

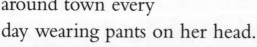

"Well, Henry, today is your lucky
day," said Miss Battle-Axe, pulling
something pink and lacy out of her
pocket. "I found these in the boys'
toilets."

"Take them away!" screamed Horrid
Henry.

3

HORRID HENRY'S SICK DAY

Cough! Cough!

Sneeze! Sneeze!

"Are you all right, Peter?" asked Mum.

Peter coughed, choked, and spluttered.

"I'm OK," he gasped.

"Are you sure?" said Dad. "You don't look very well."

"It's nothing," said Perfect Peter, coughing.

Mum felt Peter's sweaty brow.

"You've got a temperature," said Mum. "I think you'd better stay home from school today."

"But I don't want to miss school," said Peter.

"Go back to bed," said Mum.

"But I want to go to school," wailed Peter. "I'm sure I'll be—" Peter's pale, sweaty face turned green.

He dashed up the stairs to the loo. Mum ran after him.

Bleeeeeeecchhhh. The horrible sound of vomiting filled the house.

Horrid Henry stopped eating his toast. Peter, stay at home? Peter, miss school? Peter, laze about watching TV while he, Henry, had to suffer a long hard day with Miss Battle-Axe?

No way! He was sick, too. Hadn't he coughed twice this morning? And he had definitely sneezed

128

last night. Now that he thought about it, he could feel those flu germs invading. Yup, there they were, marching down his throat.

Stomp stomp stomp marched the germs. Mercy! shrieked his throat. Ha ha ha gloated the germs.

Horrid Henry thought about those spelling words he hadn't learnt. The map he hadn't finished colouring. The book report he hadn't done.

Oww. His throat hurt.

Oooh. His tummy hurt.

Eeek. His head hurt.

Yippee! He was sick!

So what would it be?

Maths or Mutant Max?

Reading or relaxing?

Commas or comics?

Tests or TV?

Hmmm, thought Horrid Henry. Hard choice.

Cough. Cough.

Dad continued reading the paper.

COUGH! COUGH! COUGH!
COUGH! COUGH!

"Are you all right, Henry?" asked Dad, without looking up.

"No!" gasped Henry. "I'm sick, too. I can't go to school."

Slowly Dad put down his newspaper.

"You don't look ill, Henry," said Dad.

"But I am," whimpered Horrid Henry. He clutched his throat. "My throat really hurts," he moaned. Then he added a few coughs, just in case.

"I feel weak," he groaned. "Everything aches."

Dad sighed.

"All right, you can stay home," he said.

Yes! thought Horrid Henry. He was amazed. It usually took much more moaning and groaning before his mean, horrible parents decided he was sick enough to miss a day of school.

"But no playing on the computer," said Dad. "If you're sick, you have to lie down."

Horrid Henry was outraged.

"But it makes me feel better to play on the computer," he protested.

"If you're well enough to play on the computer, you're well enough to go to school," said Dad.

Rats.

Oh well, thought Horrid Henry. He'd get his duvet, lie on the sofa and watch loads of TV instead. Then Mum would

bring him cold drinks, lunch on a tray, maybe even ice cream. It was always such a waste when you were too sick to enjoy being sick, thought Horrid Henry happily.

He could hear Mum and Dad arguing upstairs.

"I need to go to work," said Mum.

"I need to go to work," said Dad.

"I stayed home last time," said Mum.

"No you didn't, I did," said Dad.

"Are you sure?" said Mum.

"Yes," said Dad.

"Are you sure you're sure?" said Mum.

Horrid Henry could hardly believe his ears. Imagine arguing over who got to stay home! When he was grown-up he was going to stay home full time, testing computer games for a million pounds a week.

He bounced into the sitting room. Then he stopped bouncing. A horrible, ugly, snotty creature was stretched out

under a duvet in the comfy black chair.
Horrid Henry glanced at the TV.
A dreadful assortment of wobbling
creatures were dancing and prancing.

TRA LA LA LA LA,
WE LIVE AT NELLIE'S
WE'VE ALL GOT BIG BELLIES
WE EAT PURPLE JELLIES
AT NELLIE'S NURSERY (tee hee)

Horrid Henry sat down on the sofa.

"I want to watch *Robot Rebels*," said
Henry.

"I'm watching *Nellie's Nursery*," said
Peter, sniffing.

"Stop sniffing," said Henry.

"I can't help it, my nose is running,"
said Peter.

"I'm sicker than you, and *I'm* not
sniffing," said Henry.

"I'm sicker than you," said Peter.

"Faker."

"Faker."

"Liar."

"Liar!"

"MUM!" shrieked Henry and Peter.

Mum came into the room, carrying a tray of cold drinks and two thermometers.

"Henry's being mean to me!" whined Peter.

"Peter's being mean to *me*!" whined Henry.

"If you're well enough to fight, you're well enough to go to school, Henry," said Mum, glaring at him.

"I wasn't fighting, Peter was," said Henry.

"Henry was," said Peter, coughing.

Henry coughed louder.

Peter groaned.

Henry groaned louder.

"Uggghhhhh," moaned Peter.

"Uggghhhhhhhhh," moaned Henry. "It's not fair. I want to watch *Robot Rebels*."

"I want to watch *Nellie's Nursery*," whimpered Peter.

"Peter will choose what to watch because he's the sickest," said Mum.

Peter, sicker than he was? As if. Well, no way was Henry's sick day going to be ruined by his horrible brother.

"I'm the sickest, Mum," protested Henry. "I just don't complain so much."

Mum looked tired. She popped one thermometer into Henry's mouth and the other into Peter's.

135

"I'll be back in five minutes to check them," she said. "And I don't want to hear another peep from either of you," she added, leaving the room.

Horrid Henry lay back weakly on the sofa with the thermometer in his mouth. He felt terrible. He touched his forehead. He was burning! His temperature must be 105!

I bet my temperature is so high the thermometer won't even have enough numbers, thought Henry. Just wait till Mum saw how ill he was. Then she'd be sorry she'd been so mean.

Perfect Peter started groaning. "I'm going to be sick," he gasped, taking the thermometer from his mouth and running from the room.

The moment Peter left, Henry leapt up from the sofa and checked Peter's thermometer. 101 degrees! Oh no, Peter had a temperature. Now Peter would

start getting *all* the attention. Mum
would make Henry fetch and carry for
him. Peter might even get extra ice
cream.

Something had to be done.

Quickly Henry plunged
Peter's thermometer into
the glass of iced water.

Beep. Beep. Horrid
Henry took out his own
thermometer. It read 98.6F.
Normal.

Normal! His temperature was normal?
That was impossible. How could his
temperature be normal when he was
so ill?

If Mum saw that normal
temperature she'd have him
dressed for school in three
seconds. Obviously there
was something wrong with
that stupid thermometer.

Horrid Henry held it to the light bulb. Just to warm it up a little, he thought.

Clump. Clump.

Yikes! Mum was coming back.

Quickly Henry yanked Peter's thermometer out of the iced water and replaced his own in his mouth. Oww! It was hot.

"Let's see if you have a temperature," said Mum. She took the thermometer out of Henry's mouth.

"127 degrees!" she shrieked.

Oops.

"The thermometer must be broken," mumbled Henry. "But I still have a temperature. I'm boiling."

"Hmmn," said Mum, feeling Henry's forehead.

Peter came back into the sitting room slowly. His face was ashen.

"Check *my* temperature, Mum," said

Peter. He lay back weakly on the pillows.

Mum checked Peter's thermometer.

"57 degrees!" she shrieked.

Oops, thought Horrid Henry.

"That one must be broken too," said Henry.

He decided to change the subject fast.

"Mum, could you open the curtains please?" said Henry.

"But I want them closed," said Peter.

"Open!"

"Closed!"

"We'll leave them closed," said Mum.

Peter sneezed.

"Mum!" wailed Henry. "Peter got snot all over me."

"Mum!" wailed Peter. "Henry's smelly."

Horrid Henry glared at Peter.

Perfect Peter glared at Henry.

Henry whistled.

Peter hummed.

"Henry's whistling!"

"Peter's humming!"

"MUM!" they screamed. "Make him stop!"

"That's enough!" shouted Mum. "Go to your bedrooms, both of you!"

Henry and Peter heaved their heavy bones upstairs to their rooms.

"It's all your fault," said Henry.

"It's yours," said Peter.

The front door opened. Dad came in. He looked pale.

"I'm not feeling well," said Dad. "I'm going to bed."

Horrid Henry was bored. Horrid Henry was fed up. What was the point of being sick if you couldn't watch TV and you couldn't play on the computer?

"I'm hungry!" complained Horrid Henry.

"I'm thirsty," complained Perfect Peter.

"I'm achy," complained Dad.

"My bed's too hot!" moaned Horrid Henry.

"My bed's too cold," moaned Perfect Peter.

"My bed's too hot and too cold," moaned Dad.

Mum ran up the stairs.

Mum ran down the stairs.

"Ice cream!" shouted Horrid Henry.

"Hot water bottle!" shouted Perfect Peter.

"More pillows!" shouted Dad.

Mum walked up the stairs.

Mum walked down the stairs.

"Toast!" shouted Henry.

"Tissues!" croaked Peter.

"Tea!" gasped Dad.

"Can you wait a minute?" said Mum. "I need to sit down."

"NO!" shouted Henry, Peter, and Dad.

"All right," said Mum.

She plodded up the stairs.

She plodded down the stairs.

"My head is hurting!"

"My throat is hurting!"

"My stomach is hurting!"

Mum trudged up the stairs.

Mum trudged down the stairs.

"Crisps," screeched Henry.

"Throat lozenge," croaked Peter.

"Hankie," wheezed Dad.

Mum staggered up the stairs.

Mum staggered down the stairs.

Then Horrid Henry saw the time. Three-thirty. School was finished! The weekend was here! It was amazing, thought Horrid Henry, how much better he suddenly felt.

Horrid Henry threw off his duvet and leapt out of bed.

"Mum!" he shouted. "I'm feeling much better. Can I go and play on the computer now?"

Mum staggered into his room.

"Thank goodness you're better, Henry," she whispered. "I feel terrible. I'm going to bed. Could you bring me a cup of tea?"

What?

"I'm busy," snapped Henry.

Mum glared at him.

"All right," said Henry, grudgingly. Why couldn't Mum get her own tea? She had legs, didn't she?

Horrid Henry escaped into the sitting room. He sat down at the computer and loaded "Intergalactic Robot Rebellion: This Time It's Personal". Bliss. He'd zap some robots, then have a go at "Snake Master's Revenge".

"Henry!" gasped Mum. "Where's my tea?"

"Henry!" rasped Dad. "Bring me a drink of water!"

"Henry!" whimpered Peter. "Bring me an extra blanket."

Horrid Henry scowled. Honestly, how was he meant to concentrate with all these interruptions?

"Tea!"

"Water!"

"Blanket!"

"Get it yourself!" he howled. What was he, a servant?

"Henry!" spluttered Dad. "Come up here this minute."

Slowly, Horrid Henry got to his feet. He looked longingly at the flashing screen. But what choice did he have?

"I'm sick too!" shrieked Horrid Henry. "I'm going back to bed."

4

HORRID HENRY'S THANK YOU LETTER

Ahh! This was the life! A sofa, a telly, a bag of crisps. Horrid Henry sighed happily.

"Henry!" shouted Mum from the kitchen. "Are you watching TV?"

Henry blocked his ears. Nothing was going to interrupt his new favourite TV programme, *Terminator Gladiator*.

"Answer me, Henry!" shouted Mum. "Have you written your Christmas thank you letters?"

"NO!" bellowed Henry.

"Why not?" screamed Mum.

"Because I haven't," said Henry. "I'm busy." Couldn't she leave him alone for two seconds?

Mum marched into the room and switched off the TV.

"Hey!" said Henry. "I'm watching *Terminator Gladiator*."

"Too bad," said Mum. "I told you, no TV until you've written your thank you letters."

"It's not fair!" wailed Henry.

"I've written all *my* thank you letters," said Perfect Peter.

"Well done, Peter," said Mum. "Thank goodness *one* of my children has good manners."

Peter smiled modestly. "I always write mine the moment I unwrap a present. I'm a good boy, aren't I?"

"The best," said Mum.

"Oh, shut up, Peter," snarled Henry.

"Mum! Henry told me to shut up!" said Peter.

"Stop being horrid, Henry. You will

write to Aunt Ruby, Great-Aunt Greta and Grandma now."

"Now?" moaned Henry. "Can't I do it later?"

"When's later?" said Dad.

"Later!" said Henry. Why wouldn't they stop nagging him about those stupid letters?

Horrid Henry hated writing thank you letters. Why should he waste his precious time saying thank you for presents? Time he could be spending reading comics, or watching TV. But no. He would barely unwrap a present before Mum started nagging. She even expected him to write to Great-Aunt Greta and thank her for the Baby Poopie Pants doll. Great Aunt-Greta for one did not deserve a thank you letter.

This year Aunt Ruby had sent him a hideous lime green cardigan.

Why should he thank her for that? True, Grandma had given him £15, which was great. But then Mum had to spoil it by making him write her a letter too. Henry hated writing letters for nice presents every bit as much as he hated writing them for horrible ones.

"You have to write thank you letters," said Dad.

"But why?" said Henry.

"Because it's polite," said Dad.

"Because people have spent time and money on you," said Mum.

So what? thought Horrid Henry. Grown-ups had loads of time to do

150

whatever they wanted. No one told them, stop watching TV and write a thank you letter. Oh no. They could do it whenever they felt like it. Or not even do it at all.

And adults had tons of money compared to him. Why shouldn't they spend it buying him presents?

"All you have to do is write one page," said Dad. "What's the big deal?"

Henry stared at him. Did Dad have no idea how long it would take him to write one whole page? Hours and hours and hours.

"You're the meanest, most horrible parents in the world and I hate you!" shrieked Horrid Henry.

"Go to your room, Henry!" shouted Dad.

"And don't come down until you've written those letters," shouted Mum. "I am sick and tired of arguing about this."

Horrid Henry stomped upstairs.

151

Well, no way was he writing any thank you letters. He'd rather starve. He'd rather die. He'd stay in his room for a month. A year. One day Mum and Dad would come up to check on him and all they'd find would be a few bones. Then they'd be sorry.

Actually, knowing them, they'd probably just moan about the mess. And then Peter would be all happy because he'd get Henry's room and Henry's room was bigger.

Well, no way would he give them the satisfaction. All right, thought Horrid Henry. Dad said to write one page. Henry would write one page. In his biggest, most gigantic handwriting, Henry wrote:

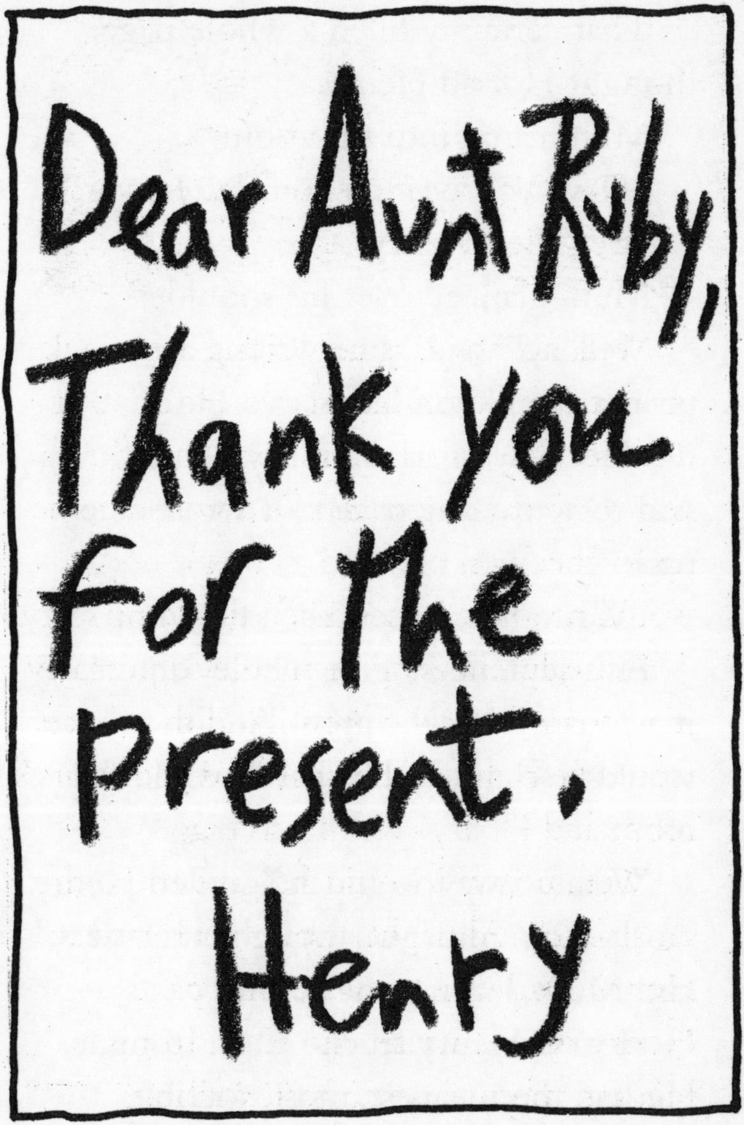

Dear Aunt Ruby,
Thank you
for the
present.
Henry

That certainly filled a whole page, thought Horrid Henry.

Mum came into the room.

"Have you written your letters yet?"

"Yes," lied Henry.

Mum glanced over his shoulder.

"Henry!" said Mum. "That is not a proper thank you letter."

"Yes it is," snarled Henry. "Dad said to write one page so I wrote one page."

"Write five sentences," said Mum.

Five sentences? Five whole sentences? It was completely impossible for anyone to write so much. His hand would fall off.

"That's way too much," wailed Henry.

"No TV until you write your letters," said Mum, leaving the room.

Horrid Henry stuck out his tongue. He had the meanest, most horrible parents in the world. When he was king

any parent who even whispered the
words "thank you letter" would get fed to
the crocodiles.

They wanted five sentences? He'd give
them five sentences. Henry picked up his
pencil and scrawled:

Dear Aunt Ruby,
No thank you for the horrible present.
It is the worst present I have ever had.
Anyway, didn't some old Roman say it
was better to give than to receive? So in
fact, you should be writing me a thank
you letter.
Henry
P.S. Next time just send money.

There! Five whole sentences. Perfect,
thought Horrid Henry. Mum said he
had to write a five sentence thank you
letter. She never said it had to be a *nice*
thank you letter. Suddenly Henry felt

quite cheerful. He folded the letter and popped it in the stamped envelope Mum had given him.

One down. Two to go.

In fact, Aunt Ruby's no thank you letter would do just fine for Great-Aunt Greta. He'd just substitute Great-Aunt Greta's name for Aunt Ruby's and copy the rest.

Bingo. Another letter was done.

Now, Grandma. She *had* sent money so he'd have to write something nice.

"Thank you for the money, blah blah blah, best present I've ever received, blah blah blah, next year send more money, £15 isn't very much, Ralph got £20 from *his* grandma, blah blah blah."

What a waste, thought Horrid Henry as he signed it and put it in the envelope, to spend so much time on a letter, only to have to write the same old thing all over again next year.

And then suddenly Horrid Henry had a wonderful, spectacular idea. Why had he never thought of this before? He would be rich, rich, rich. "There goes money-bags Henry," kids would whisper enviously, as he swaggered down the street followed by Peter lugging a hundred videos for Henry to watch in his mansion on one of his twenty-eight giant TVs. Mum and Dad and Peter would be living in their hovel somewhere, and if they were very, very nice to him Henry *might* let them watch one of his smaller TVs for fifteen minutes or so once a month.

Henry was going to start a business. A business guaranteed to make him rich.

"Step right up, step right up," said Horrid Henry. He was wearing a sign saying: HENRY'S THANK YOU LETTERS: "Personal letters written just for you." A small crowd of children gathered round him.

"I'll write all your thank you letters for you," said Henry. "All you have to do

is to give me a stamped, addressed envelope and tell me what present you got. I'll do the rest."

"How much for a thank you letter?" asked Kung-Fu Kate.

"£1," said Henry.

"No way," said Greedy Graham.

"99p," said Henry.

"Forget it," said Lazy Linda.

"OK, 50p," said Henry. "And two for 75p."

"Done," said Linda.

Henry opened his notebook. "And what were the presents?" he asked. Linda made a face. "Handkerchiefs," she spat. "And a bookmark."

"I can do a 'no thank you' letter," said Henry. "I'm very good at those."

Linda considered.

"Tempting," she said, "but then mean Uncle John won't send something better next time."

Business was brisk. Dave bought three.
Ralph bought four "no thank you"s.
Even Moody Margaret bought one.
Whoopee, thought Horrid Henry. His
pockets were jingle-jangling with cash.
Now all he had to do was to write
seventeen letters. Henry tried not to
think about that.

The moment he got home from
school Henry went straight to his room.
Right, to work, thought Henry. His heart
sank as he looked at the blank pages. All
those letters! He would be here for
weeks. Why had he ever set up a letter-
writing business?

But then Horrid Henry thought.
True, he'd promised a personal letter
but how would Linda's aunt ever find
out that Margaret's granny had received
the same one? She wouldn't! If he used
the computer, it would be a cinch. And
it would be a letter sent personally,

thought Henry, because I am a
person and I will personally print it
out and send it. All he'd have to do
was to write the names at the top and
to sign them. Easy-peasy lemon
squeezy.

Then again, all that signing. And
writing all those names at the top.
And separating the thank you letters
from the no thank you ones.

Maybe there was a better way.

Horrid Henry sat down at the
computer and typed:

Dear Sir or Madam,

That should cover everyone, thought
Henry, and I won't have to write anyone's
name.

Thank you/No thank you for the
a) wonderful

b) horrible

c) disgusting

present. I really loved it/hated it. In fact, it is the best present/worst present I have ever received. I played with it/broke it/ate it/spent it/threw it in the bin straight away. Next time just send lots of money.

Best wishes/worst wishes

Now, how to sign it? Aha, thought Henry.

Your friend or relative.

Perfect, thought Horrid Henry. Sir or Madam knows whether they deserve a thank you or a no thank you letter. Let them do some work for a change and tick the correct answers.

Print.

Print.

Print.

Out spewed seventeen letters. It only took a moment to stuff them in the envelopes. He'd pop the letters in the postbox on the way to school.

Had an easier way to become a millionaire ever been invented, thought Horrid Henry, as he turned on the telly?

Ding dong.

It was two weeks after Henry set up "Henry's Thank You Letters."

Horrid Henry opened the door.

A group of Henry's customers stood there, waving pieces of paper and shouting.

"My granny sent the letter back and now I can't watch TV for a week," wailed Moody Margaret.

"I'm grounded!" screamed Aerobic Al.

"I have to go swimming!" screamed Lazy Linda.

"No sweets!" yelped Greedy Graham.

"No pocket money!" screamed Rude Ralph.

"And it's all your fault!" they shouted.

Horrid Henry glared at his angry customers. He was outraged. After all his hard work, *this* was the thanks he got?

"Too bad!" said Horrid Henry as he slammed the door. Honestly, there was no pleasing some people.

"Henry," said Mum. "I just had the
strangest phone call from Aunt Ruby . . ."

HORRID
HENRY
MEETS THE
QUEEN

For my childhood friends
Tootie Ackerman-Hicks and Dinah Manoff

CONTENTS

1

HORRID HENRY'S CHORES

The weekend! The lovely, lovely weekend. Sleeping in. Breakfast in his pyjamas. Morning TV. Afternoon TV. Evening TV. No school and no Miss Battle-Axe for two whole days.

In fact, there was only one bad thing about the weekend. Henry didn't even want to think about it. Maybe Mum would forget, he thought hopefully. Maybe today would be the day she didn't burst in and ruin everything.

Horrid Henry settled down in the comfy black chair and switched on his new favourite TV show, *Hog House*, where teenagers competed to see whose room was the most disgusting.

Henry couldn't wait till he was a terrible teen too. His bedroom would surely beat anything ever seen on *Hog House*.

"Eeeew," squealed Horrid Henry happily, as Filthy Phil showed off what he kept under his bed.

"Yuck!" shrieked Horrid Henry, as Mouldy Myra yanked open her cupboard.

"Oooh, gross!" howled Horrid Henry, as Tornado Tariq showed why his family had moved out.

"And this week's winner for the most revolting room is—"

CLUNK

CLUNK

CLUNK

Mum clanked in. She was dragging her favourite instruments of torture: a hoover and a duster. Peter followed.

"Henry, turn off that horrid programme

this minute," said Mum. "It's time to do
your chores."

"NO!" screamed Horrid Henry.

Was there a more hateful, horrible word
in the world than chores? *Chores* was
worse than *homework*. Worse than *vegetables*.
Even worse than *injection*, *share,* and
bedtime. When he was King no child would
ever have to do chores. Any parent who so
much as whispered the word *chores* would
get catapulted over the battlements into
the piranha-infested moat.

"You can start by picking up your dirty
socks from the floor," said Mum.

Pick up a sock? Pick up a sock? Was there no end to Mum's meanness? Who cared if he had a few old socks scattered around the place?

"I can't believe you're making me do this!" screamed Henry. He glared at Mum. Then he glared at his crumpled socks. The socks were miles away from the sofa. He'd pick them up later. Much later.

"Henry, your turn to hoover the sitting room," said Mum. "Peter, your turn to dust."

"No!" howled Horrid Henry. "I'm allergic to hoovers."

Mum ignored him.

"Then empty the bins and put the dirty clothes into the washing machine. And make sure you separate the whites from the coloureds."

Henry didn't move.

"It will only take fifteen minutes," said Mum.

"It's not fair!" wailed Henry. "I hoovered last week."

"No you didn't, I did," said Peter.

"I did!" screamed Henry.

"Liar!"

"Liar!"

"Can't I do it later?" said Horrid Henry. Later had such a happy way of turning into never.

"N-O spells no," said Mum.

Peter started dusting the TV.

"Stop it!" said Henry. "I'm watching."

"I'm dusting," said Peter.

"Out of my way, worm," hissed Horrid Henry.

Mum marched over and switched off the TV. "No TV until you do your chores, Henry. Everyone has to pitch in and help in this family."

Horrid Henry was outraged. Why should he help around the house? That was his lazy parents' job. Didn't he work hard enough already, heaving his heavy bones to school every day?

And all the schoolwork he did! It was amazing, thought Horrid Henry, as he lay kicking and screaming on the sofa, that he was still alive.

"I WON'T! I'M NOT YOUR SLAVE!"

"Henry, it's not fair if Mum and Dad do *all* the housework," said Perfect Peter.

That seemed fair to Henry.

"Quite right, Peter," said Mum, beaming. "What a lovely thoughtful boy you are."

"Shut up, Peter!" screamed Henry.

"Don't be horrid, Henry!" screamed Mum.

"No TV and no pocket money until you do your chores," said Dad, running in.

Henry stopped screaming.

No pocket money! No TV!

"I don't need any pocket money," shrieked Henry.

"Fine," said Mum.

Wait, what was he saying?

Of course he needed pocket money. How else would he buy sweets? And he'd die if he couldn't watch TV.

"I'm calling the police," said Horrid Henry. "They'll come and arrest you for child cruelty."

"Finished!" sang out Perfect Peter. "I've done all *my* chores," he added, "can I have my pocket money please?"

"Of course you can," said Mum. She handed Peter a shiny 50p piece.

Horrid Henry glared at Peter. Could that ugly toad get any uglier?

"All right," snarled Henry. "I'll hoover.

And out of my way, frog face, or I'll hoover you up."

"Mum!" wailed Peter. "Henry's trying to hoover me."

"Just do your chores, Henry," said Mum. She felt tired.

"You could have done *all* your chores in the time you've spent arguing," said Dad. He felt tired, too.

Henry slammed the sitting room door behind his mean horrible parents. He looked at the hoover with loathing. Why didn't that stupid machine just hoover by itself? A robot hoover, that's what he needed.

Henry switched it on.

VROOM!
VROOM!

"Hoover, hoover!" ordered Henry.

The hoover did not move.

"Go on, hoover, you can do it," said Henry.

VROOM! VROOM! Still the hoover didn't move.

What a lot of noise that stupid machine makes, thought Henry. I bet you can hear it all over the house.

And then suddenly Horrid Henry had a brilliant, spectacular idea. Why had he never thought of it before? He'd ask to hoover every week.

Henry dragged the hoover over to the sitting room door and left it roaring there. Then he flopped on the sofa and switched on the TV. Great, *Hog House* hadn't finished!

VROOMVROOMVROOM

Mum and Dad listened to the hoover blaring from the sitting room. Goodness, Henry was working hard. They were amazed.

"Isn't Henry doing a good job," said Mum.

"He's been working over thirty minutes non-stop," said Dad.

"Finally, he's being responsible," said Mum.

"At last," said Dad.

"Go Tariq!" cheered Henry, as Tornado Tariq blew into his parents' tidy bedroom. Ha ha ha, chortled Henry, what a shock those parents would get.

"Stay tuned for the Filthy Final between Tariq and Myra, coming up in three minutes!" said the presenter, Dirty Dirk.

Footsteps. Yikes, someone was coming.
Oh no.

Henry sprang from the sofa, turned off
the telly and grabbed the hoover.

Mum walked in.

Horrid Henry began to pant.

"I've worked so hard, Mum," gasped
Henry. "Please can I stop now?"

Mum stared at the dustballs covering the
carpet.

"But Henry," said Mum. "There's still
dust everywhere."

"I can't help it," said Henry. "I did my
best."

"All right, Henry," said Mum, sighing.

YES! thought Horrid Henry.

"But remember, no TV until you've
emptied the bins and separated the
laundry."

"I know, I know," muttered Henry,
running up the stairs. If he finished his

chores in the next two minutes, he'd be in
time for the *Hog House* final!

Right. Mum said to empty the bins. She
didn't say into what, just that the bins had
to be empty.

It was the work
of a few moments
to tip all the
wastepaper baskets
onto the floor.

That's done, thought
Horrid Henry, racing
down the stairs. Now that
stupid laundry. When he was a billionaire
computer game tester, he'd never wash his
clothes. He'd just buy new ones.

Horrid Henry glared at the dirty clothes
piled on the floor in front of the washing
machine. It would take him hours to
separate the whites from the coloureds.
What a waste of his valuable time, thought
Henry. Mum and Dad just made him do it

to be mean. What difference could it make to wash a red sweatshirt with a white sheet? None.

Horrid Henry shoved all the clothes into the washing machine and slammed the door.

Free at last.

"Done!" shrieked Horrid Henry.

Wow, what a brilliant *Hog House* that was, thought Horrid Henry, jingling his pocket money. He wandered past the washing machine. Strange, he didn't remember all those pink clothes swirling around. Since when did his family have pink sheets and pink towels?

Since he'd washed a red sweatshirt with the whites.

Uh oh.

Mum would be furious. Dad would be furious. His punishment would be terrible. Hide! thought Horrid Henry.

★

Dad stared at his newly pink underpants, shirts, and vests.

Mum stared at her best white skirt, now her worst pink one.

Henry stared at the floor. This time there was no escape.

"Maybe we're asking too much of you," said Dad, gazing at the trail of rubbish lying round the house.

"You're just not responsible enough," said Mum.

"Too clumsy," said Dad.

"Too young," said Mum.

"Maybe it's easier if we do the chores ourselves," said Dad.

"Maybe it is," said Mum.

Horrid Henry could hardly believe his ears. No more chores? Because he was so bad at doing them?

"Yippee!" squealed Henry.

"On the other hand, maybe not," said Dad, glaring. "We'll see how well you do your chores next week."

"Okay," said Horrid Henry agreeably.

He had the feeling his chore-doing skills wouldn't be improving.

2

....

MOODY MARGARET
CASTS A SPELL

"You are getting sleepy," said Moody
Margaret. "You are getting very sleepy . . ."

Slowly she waved her watch in front of
Susan.

"So sleepy . . . you are now asleep . . . you
are now fast asleep . . ."

"No I'm not," said Sour Susan.

"When I click my fingers you will start
snoring."

Margaret clicked her fingers.

"But I'm not asleep," said Susan.

Margaret glared at her.

"How am I supposed to hypnotise you if
you don't try?" said Margaret.

"I *am* trying, you're just a bad hypnotist,"

said Susan sourly. "Now it's my turn."

"No it's not, it's still mine," said Margaret.

"You've had your go," said Susan.

"No I haven't!"

"But I never get to be the hypnotist!" wailed Susan.

"Cry baby!"

"Meanie!"

"Cheater!"

"Cheater!"

Slap!

Slap!

Susan glared at Margaret. Why was she friends with such a mean moody bossyboots?

Margaret glared at Susan. Why was she friends with such a stupid sour sulker?

"I hate you, Margaret!" screamed Sour Susan.

"I hate you more!" screamed Moody Margaret.

188

"Shut up, landlubbers!" shrieked Horrid Henry from his hammock in the garden next door. "Or the Purple Hand will make you walk the plank!"

"Shut up yourself, Henry," said Margaret.

"Yeah, Henry," said Susan.

"You are stupid, you are stupid," chanted Rude Ralph, who was playing pirates with Henry.

"You're the stupids," snapped Moody Margaret. "Now leave us alone, we're busy."

"Henry, can I play pirates with you?" asked Perfect Peter, wandering out from the house.

"No, you puny prawn!" screamed Captain Hook. "Out of my way before I tear you to pieces with my hook!"

"Muuum," wailed Peter. "Henry said he was going to tear me to pieces!"

"Stop being horrid, Henry!" shouted Mum.

"And he won't let me play with him," said Peter.

"Can't you be nice to your brother for once?" said Dad.

NO! thought Horrid Henry. Why should he be nice to that tell-tale brat?

Horrid Henry did not want to play pirates with Peter. Peter was the world's worst pirate. He couldn't swordfight. He couldn't swashbuckle. He couldn't remember pirate curses. All he could do was whine.

"Okay, Peter, you're the prisoner. Wait in the fort," said Henry.

"But I'm always the prisoner," said Peter.

Henry glared at him.

"Do you want to play or don't you?"

"Yes Captain," said Peter. He crawled into the lair of the Purple Hand. Being prisoner was better than nothing, he supposed. He just hoped he wouldn't have to wait too long.

"Let's get out of here quick," Henry whispered to Rude Ralph. "I've got a great idea for playing a trick on Margaret and Susan." He whispered to Ralph. Ralph grinned.

Horrid Henry hoisted himself onto the low brick wall between his garden and Margaret's.

Moody Margaret was still waving her watch at Susan. Unfortunately, Susan had her back turned and her arms folded.

"Go away, Henry," ordered Margaret.

"Yeah Henry," said Susan. "No boys."

"Are you being hypnotists?" said Henry.

"Margaret's trying to hypnotise me, only she can't 'cause she's a rubbish hypnotist," said Susan.

"That's your fault," said Margaret, glaring.

"Of course you can't hypnotise her," said Henry. "You're doing it all wrong."

"And what would you know about that?" asked Margaret.

"Because," said Horrid Henry, "I am a master hypnotist."

Moody Margaret laughed.

"He is too a master hypnotist," said Ralph. "He hypnotises me all the time."

"Oh yeah?" said Margaret.

"Yeah," said Henry.

"Prove it," said Margaret.

"Okay," said Horrid Henry. "Gimme the watch."

Margaret handed it over.

He turned to Ralph.

"Look into my eyes," he ordered.

Ralph looked into Henry's eyes.

"Now watch the watch," ordered Henry the hypnotist, swinging the watch back and forth. Rude Ralph swayed.

"You will obey my commands," said Henry.

"I– will – obey," said Ralph in a robot voice.

"When I whistle, you will jump off the

wall," said Henry. He whistled.

Ralph jumped off the wall.

"See?" said Horrid Henry.

"That doesn't prove he's hypnotised," said Margaret. "You have to make him do silly things."

"Like what?" said Henry.

"Tell him he's got no clothes on."

"Ralph, you're a nudie," said Henry.

Ralph immediately started running round the garden shrieking.

"Aaaaaaarrgghh!" yelped Ralph. "I'm a nudie! I'm a nudie! Give me some clothes, help help! No one look, I'm naked!"

Margaret hesitated. There was no way Henry could have *really* hypnotised Ralph – was there?

"I still don't believe he's hypnotised," said Margaret.

"Then watch this," said Horrid Henry. "Ralph – when I snap my fingers you will be ... Margaret."

Snap!

"My name is Margaret," said Ralph. "I'm a mean bossyboots. I'm the biggest bossiest boot. I'm a frogface."

Margaret blushed red.

Susan giggled.

"It's not funny," snapped Margaret. *No one* made fun of her and lived to tell the tale.

"See?" said Henry. "He obeys my every command."

"Wow," said Susan. "You really are a hypnotist. Can you teach me?"

"Maybe," said Horrid Henry. "How much will you pay me?"

"He's just a big faker," said Margaret. She stuck her nose in the air. "If you're such a

195

great hypnotist, then hypnotise *me*."

Oops. Now he was trapped. Margaret was trying to spoil his trick. Well, no way would he let her.

Horrid Henry remembered who he was. The boy who got Miss Battle-Axe sent to the head. The boy who terrified the bogey babysitter. The boy who tricked the Tooth Fairy. He could hypnotise Margaret any day.

"Sure," he said, waving the watch in front of Margaret.

"You are getting sleepy," droned Henry. "You are getting very sleepy. When I snap

my fingers you will obey my every command."

Henry snapped his fingers. Margaret glared at him.

"Well?" said Moody Margaret.

"Don't you know *anything*?" said Horrid Henry. He thought fast. "That was just the beginning bit. I will complete part two once I have freed Ralph from my power. Ralph, repeat after me, 'I am sellotape'."

"I am sellotape," said Rude Ralph. Then he belched.

"I am burping sellotape," said Rude Ralph. He caught Henry's eye. They burst out laughing.

"Ha ha, Susan, fooled you!" shrieked Henry.

"Did not," shrieked Susan.

"Did too. Nah nah ne nah nah!" Henry and Ralph ran round Margaret, whooping and cheering.

"Come on Margaret," said Susan. "Let's

go do some *real* hypnosis."

Margaret didn't move.

"Come on, Margaret," said Susan.

"I am sellotape," said Margaret.

"No you're not," said Susan.

"Yes I am," said Margaret.

Henry and Ralph stopped whooping.

"There's something wrong with
Margaret," said Susan. "She's acting all
funny. Margaret, are you okay? Margaret?
Margaret?"

Moody Margaret stood very still. Her
eyes looked blank.

Horrid Henry snapped his
fingers.

"Raise your right arm,"
he ordered.

Margaret raised her
right arm.

Huh? thought Horrid Henry.

"Pinch Susan."

Margaret pinched Susan.

"Owww!" yelped Susan.

"Repeat after me, 'I am a stupid girl'."

"I am a stupid girl," said Margaret.

"No you're not," said Susan.

"Yes I am," said Margaret.

"She's hypnotised," said Horrid Henry. He'd actually hypnotised Moody Margaret. This was amazing. This was fantastic. He really truly was a master hypnotist!

"Will you obey me, slave?"

"I will obey," said Margaret.

"When I click my fingers, you will be a ...chicken."

Click!

"Squawk! Squawk! Squawk!" cackled Margaret, flapping her arms wildly.

"What have you done to her?" wailed Sour Susan.

"Wow," said Rude Ralph. "You've hypnotised her."

Horrid Henry could not believe his luck. If he could hypnotise Margaret, he could hypnotise anyone. Everyone would have to obey his commands. He would be master of the world! The universe! Everything!

Henry could see it now.

"Henry, ten out of ten," Miss Battle-Axe would say. "Henry is so clever he doesn't ever need to do homework again."

Oh boy, would he fix Miss Battle-Axe.

He'd make her do the hula in a grass skirt when she wasn't running round the playground mooing like a cow.

He'd make the head Mrs Oddbod just have chocolate and cake for school dinners. And no P.E. – ever. In fact,

he'd make Mrs Oddbod close down the
school.

And as for Mum and Dad ...

"Henry, have as many sweets as you like,"
Dad would say.

"No bedtime for you," Mum would say.

"Henry, watch as much TV as you want,"
Dad would say.

"Henry, here's your pocket money –

£1000 a week. Tell us if you need more,"
Mum would smile.

"Peter, go to your room and stay there
for a year!" Mum and Dad would scream.

Henry would hypnotise them all later.
But first, what should he make Margaret
do?

Ah yes. Her house was filled with sweets
and biscuits and fizzy drinks – all the
things Henry's horrible parents never let
him have.

"Bring us all your sweets, all your biscuits
and a Fizzywizz drink."

"Yes, master," said Moody Margaret.

Henry stretched out in the hammock. So
did Rude Ralph. This was the life!

Sour Susan didn't know what to do. On
the one hand, Margaret was mean and
horrible, and she hated her. It was fun
watching her obey orders for once. On the
other hand, Susan would much rather
Margaret was *her* slave than Henry's.

"Unhypnotise her, Henry," said Sour
Susan.

"Soon," said Horrid Henry.

"Let's hypnotise Peter next," said Ralph.

"Yeah," said Henry. No more telling
tales. No more goody goody vegetable-
eating I'm Mr Perfect. Oh boy would he
hypnotise Peter!

Moody Margaret came slowly out of her
house. She was carrying a large pitcher and
a huge bowl of chocolate mousse.

"Here is your Fizzywizz drink, master,"
said Margaret. Then she poured it on top
of him.

"Wha? Wha?" spluttered Henry, gasping
and choking.

"And your dinner, frogface," she added,
tipping the mousse all over Ralph.

"Ugggh!" wailed Ralph.

"NAH NAH NE NAH NAH," shrieked
Margaret. "Fooled you! Fooled you!"

Perfect Peter crept out of the Purple-

Hand Fort. What was all that yelling? It must be a pirate mutiny!

"Hang on pirates, here I come!" shrieked Peter, charging at the thrashing hammock as fast as he could.

CRASH!

A sopping wet pirate captain and a mousse-covered first mate lay on the ground. They stared up at their prisoner.

"Hi Henry," said Peter. "I mean, hi

Captain." He took a step backwards. "I mean, Lord High Excellent Majesty." He took another step back.

"Ugh, we were playing pirate mutiny – weren't we?"

"DIE, WORM!" yelled Horrid Henry, leaping up.

"MUUUUUUM!" shrieked Peter.

3

HORRID HENRY'S BATHTIME

Horrid Henry loved baths.

He loved causing great big tidal waves.

He loved making bubble-bath beards and bubble-bath hats.

He loved staging battles with Yellow Duck and Snappy Croc. He loved diving for buried treasure, fighting sea monsters, and painting the walls with soapy suds.

But best of all, being in the bath meant Peter couldn't bother him, or wreck his games or get him into trouble.

Henry stretched out in the lovely warm water. The bubbles were piled high to overflowing, just as he liked.

SLOSH

SLOSH

SLOSH

A bucketload of soapy suds cascaded onto the floor. Yippee! The first tidal wave of the day. Good thing Mum wasn't around. But then what Mum didn't know wouldn't hurt her.

Now what to do first? A Croc and Duck fight? Or the killer tidal wave?

"Heh heh heh," cackled Horrid Henry, "watch your tail, Yellow Duck, 'cause Snappy Croc is on the attack. Snap! Snap! Snap!"

Suddenly the bathroom door opened. A slimy toad slithered in.

"Oy, get out of here, Peter," said Henry.

"Dad said we had to share a bath," said Perfect Peter, taking off his shirt.

What?

"Liar!" screeched Horrid Henry. "You are dead meat!" He reached for his Super Soaker. Henry was not allowed to use it in the house, but this was an emergency.

"AAARRRGGGHHH," squealed Peter as a jet of water hit him in the face.

Dad dashed in.

"Put that Super Soaker away or I'll confiscate it," shouted Dad.

Henry's finger trembled on the trigger.

Dad's red face was so tempting . . .

Henry could see it now. POW! Dad
soaking wet. Dad screaming. Dad
snatching Super Soaker and throwing it in
the rubbish and telling Henry no TV for
ever . . .

Hmmm. Dad's red face was a little less
tempting.

"Just look at this floor, Henry," said Dad.
"What a waste of water."

"It's not a waste," said Horrid Henry,
holding tight onto his Super Soaker in case
Dad lunged, "it's a tidal wave."

"Too much water is being wasted in this

house," said Dad. "From now on you and Peter will share a bath."

Horrid Henry could not believe his ears. *Share* a bath? *Share* a bath with stupid smelly Peter?

"NOOOO," wailed Henry.

"I don't mind sharing, Dad," said Peter. "We all have to do our bit to save water."

"But Peter pees in the bath," said Henry.

"I do not," said Perfect Peter. "Henry does."

"Liar!"

"Liar!"

"And we'll be squashed!" wailed Henry. "And he likes the bath too cold ! And he—"

"That's enough Henry," said Dad. "Now make room for Peter."

Horrid Henry ducked his head under water. He was never coming back up. Never. Then they'd be sorry they made him share his bath with an ugly toad snot face telltale goody-goody poo breath . . .

GASP.

Horrid Henry came up for air.

"If you don't make room for Peter you'll be getting out now," said Dad. "And no TV for a week."

Scowling, Horrid Henry moved his legs a fraction of an inch.

"Henry ..." said Dad.

Horrid Henry moved his legs another fraction.

"I don't want to sit by the taps," said Peter. "They hurt my back."

"Well I don't want to sit there either," said Henry. "And I was here first. I'm not moving."

"Just get in, Peter," said Dad.

Perfect Peter got in the bath and sat against the taps. His lower lip trembled.

Ha ha ha, thought Horrid Henry, stretching out his legs. Peter was all squished at the yucky end of the bath. Good. Serve him right for ruining Henry's fun.

"Nah Nah Ne Nah Nah," chortled
Horrid Henry.

"Dad, the bath's too hot," moaned Peter.
"I'm boiling."

Dad added cold water.

"Too cold!" screeched Horrid Henry.
"I'm freezing!"

Dad added hot water.

"Too hot!" said Perfect Peter.

Dad sighed.

"New house rule: the person who sits by

213

the taps decides the temperature," said
Dad, letting in a trickle of cold water.
"Now I don't want to hear another peep
out of either of you," he added, closing the
door.

Horrid Henry could have punched
himself. Why hadn't he thought of that? If
he were by the taps *he'd* be the bath king.

"Move," said Henry.

"No," said Peter.

"I want to sit by the taps," said Henry.

"Too bad," said Peter. "I'm not moving."

"Make it hotter," ordered Henry.

"No," said Peter. "I control the
temperature because *I'm* sitting by the
taps."

"DAD!" shouted Henry. "Peter wants the
bath too cold!"

"MUM!" shouted Peter. "Henry wants
the bath too hot!"

"I'm freezing!"

"I'm boiling!"

"Be quiet both of you," screamed Dad from the kitchen.

Horrid Henry glared at Peter.

Perfect Peter glared at Henry.

"Move your legs," said Henry.

"I'm on my side," said Peter.

Henry kicked him.

"No you're not," said Henry.

Peter kicked him back.

Henry splashed him.

"Muuuuuuuum!" shrieked Peter. "Henry's being horrid."

"Peter's being horrid!"

"Make him stop!" shouted Henry and Peter.

"AAARRRRGHHHHHH!" screeched Peter.

"AAARRRRGHHHHHH!" screeched Henry.

"Stop fighting!" screamed Mum.

Perfect Peter picked up Yellow Duck.

"Give me Yellow Duck," hissed Henry.

"No," said Peter.

"But it's my duck!"

"Mine!"

SLAP

SLAP

"Waaaaaaah," wailed Peter. "Muuuum!"

Mum ran in. "What's going on in here?"

"He hit me!" screeched Henry and Peter.

"That's it, both of you out," said Mum.

"Bathtime, boys," said Mum the next evening.

Horrid Henry raced upstairs. This time he'd make sure he was the first one in. But

when he reached the bathroom, a terrible sight met his eyes. There was Peter, already sitting at the tap end. Henry could practically see the ice cubes floating on the freezing water.

Rats. Another bathtime ruined.

Henry stuck his toe in.

"It's too cold!" moaned Henry. "And I don't want to have a bath with Peter. I want my own bath."

"Stop making a fuss and get in," said Mum. "And no fighting. I'm leaving the door open."

Horrid Henry got into the bath.

Eeeeek! He was turning into an icicle! Well, not for long. He had a brilliant, spectacular plan.

"Stop making ripples," hissed Horrid Henry. "You have to keep the water smooth."

"I am keeping the water smooth," said Peter.

"Shh! Hold still."

"Why?" said Peter.

"I wouldn't splash if I were you," whispered Henry. "*It* doesn't like splashing."

"Why are you whispering?" said Peter.

"Because there's a monster in the tub," said Henry.

"No there isn't," said Peter.

"It's the plughole monster," said Horrid

Henry. "It sneaks up
the drains, slithers
through the
plughole and –
slurp! Down you
go."

"You big liar," said
Peter. He shifted slightly off the plughole.

Henry shrugged.

"It's up to you," he said. "Don't say I
didn't warn you when the Plughole
Monster sucks you down the drain!"

Peter scooted away from the plughole.

"MUUUUM!" he howled, jumping out
of the bath. Henry grabbed his spot,
turned on the hot water, and stretched out.
Ahhhh!

Peter continued to shriek.

"What's going on in here?" said Mum
and Dad, bursting into the bathroom.

"Henry said I was going to get sucked
down the plughole," snivelled Peter.

"Don't be horrid, Henry," said Mum.
"Get out of the bath this minute."

"But – but ... " said Horrid Henry.

"New house rules," said Mum. "From
now on *I'll* run the bath and *I'll* decide the
temperature."

We'll see about that, thought Horrid
Henry.

The next evening, Henry sneaked into the
bathroom. A thin trickle of water dribbled
from the tap. The bath was just starting to
fill. He felt the water.

Brrr! Freezing cold. Just how he hated
it. Peter must have fiddled with the temperature. Well, no way! Henry turned up the
hot tap full blast. Hot water gushed into the
bath. That's much better, thought Horrid
Henry. He smiled and went downstairs.

From his bedroom, Peter heard Henry
stomping from the bathroom. What was he

up to? When the coast was clear, Peter
tiptoed into the bathroom and dipped his
fingers in the water. Oww! Boiling hot.
Just how he hated it. Henry must have
fiddled with the temperature: Mum would
never make it so hot. Peter turned up the
cold tap full blast. Much better, thought
Peter.

Mum and Dad were sitting in the
kitchen drinking tea.

Mum smiled. "It's lovely and quiet
upstairs, isn't it?"

Dad smiled. "I knew they'd be able to
share a bath, in the end."

Mum stopped smiling.

"Do you hear something?"

Dad listened.

"Leave me alone!" screamed Henry from
the sitting room.

"You leave me alone!" screamed Peter.

"Just the usual," said Dad.

"Didn't you put them in the bath?"

Dad stopped smiling. "No. Didn't you?"
Mum looked at Dad.
Dad looked at Mum.
Plink!
Plink!
Plink!

Water began to drip from the ceiling.
"I think I hear – RUNNING WATER!"
screamed Mum. She dashed up the stairs.
Dad ran after her.
Mum opened the bathroom door.
Water gushed from the bathroom, and
roared down the stairs.

SLIP!

SLIDE!

Mum landed on her bottom.

Plop!

Dad toppled into the bath.

Splash!

"It wasn't me!" screamed Henry.

"It wasn't me!" wailed Peter. Then he burst into tears.

"Mum!" wept Peter. "I've been a bad boy."

Snap! Snap!

Snappy Croc was defending his tail. Yellow Duck was twisting round to attack. Ka-boom!

Horrid Henry lay back in the bath and closed his eyes. Mum and Dad had decided to let Henry have baths on his own. To save water, they'd take showers.

4

HORRID HENRY MEETS THE QUEEN

Perfect Peter bowed to himself in the mirror.

"Your Majesty," he said, pretending to present a bouquet. "Welcome to our school, your Majesty. My name is Peter, Your Majesty. Thank you, Your Majesty. Goodbye, Your Majesty." Slowly Perfect Peter retreated backwards, bowing and smiling.

"Oh shut up," snarled Horrid Henry. He glared at Peter. If Peter said 'Your Majesty' one more time, he would, he would – Horrid Henry wasn't sure what he'd do, but it would be horrible.

The Queen was coming to Henry's school! The real live Queen! The real live Queen, with her dogs and jewels and crowns and castles and beefeaters and knights and horses and ladies-in-waiting, was coming to see the Tudor wall they had built.

Yet for some reason Horrid Henry had not been asked to give the Queen a bouquet. Instead, the head, Mrs Oddbod, had chosen Peter.

Peter!

Why stupid smelly old ugly toad Peter? It was so unfair. Just because Peter had more stars than anyone in the 'Good as

Gold' book, was that any reason to choose *him*? Henry should have been chosen. He would do a much better job than Peter. Besides, he wanted to ask the Queen how many TVs she had. Now he'd never get the chance.

"Your Majesty," said Peter, bowing.

"Your Majesty," mimicked Henry, curtseying.

Perfect Peter ignored him. He'd been ignoring Henry a lot ever since *he'd* been chosen to meet the queen. Come to think of it, everyone had been ignoring Henry.

"Isn't it thrilling?" said Mum for the millionth time.

"Isn't it fantastic?" said Dad for the billionth time.

"NO!" Henry had said. Who'd want to hand some rotten flowers to a stupid queen anyhow? Not Horrid Henry. And he certainly didn't want to have his picture in the paper, and everyone making a fuss.

"Bow, bouquet, answer her question, walk away," muttered Perfect Peter. Then he paused. "Or is it bouquet, bow?"

Horrid Henry had had just about enough of Peter showing off.

"You're doing it all wrong," said Henry.

"No I'm not," said Peter.

"Yes you are," said Henry. "You're supposed to hold the bouquet up to her nose, so she can have a sniff before you give it to her."

Perfect Peter paused.

"No I'm not," said Peter.

Horrid Henry shook his head sadly. "I think we'd better practise," he said.

"Pretend I'm the Queen." He picked up Peter's shiny silver crown, covered in fool's jewels, and put it on his head.

Perfect Peter beamed. He'd been begging Henry to practise with him all morning. "Ask me a question the Queen would ask," said Peter.

Horrid Henry considered.

"Why are you so smelly, little boy?" said the Queen, holding her nose.

"The Queen wouldn't ask *that*!" gasped Perfect Peter.

"Yes she would," said Henry.

"Wouldn't."

"Would."

"And I'm not smelly!"

Horrid Henry waved his hand in front of his face.

"Poo!" said the Queen. "Take this smelly boy to the Tower."

"Stop it, Henry," said Peter. "Ask me a real question, like my name or what year I'm in."

"Why are you so ugly?" said the Queen.

"MUM!" wailed Peter. "Henry called me ugly. And smelly."

"Don't be horrid, Henry!" shouted Mum.

"Do you want me to practise with you or don't you?" hissed Henry.

"Practise," sniffed Peter.

"Well, go on then," said Henry.

Perfect Peter walked up to Henry and bowed.

"Wrong!" said Henry. "You don't bow to the Queen, you curtsey."

"Curtsey?" said Peter. Mrs Oddbod hadn't said anything about curtseying. "But I'm a boy."

"The law was changed," said Henry. "Everyone curtseys now."

Peter hesitated.

"Are you sure?" asked Peter.

"Yes," said Henry. "And when you meet the Queen, you put your thumb on your nose and wriggle your fingers. Like this."

Horrid Henry cocked a snook.

Perfect Peter gasped. Mrs Oddbod hadn't said anything about thumbs on noses.

"But that's . . . rude," said Perfect Peter.

"Not to the Queen," said Horrid Henry. "You can't just say 'hi' to the Queen like she's a person. She's the Queen. There are special rules. If you get it wrong she can chop off your head."

Chop off his head! Mrs Oddbod hadn't said anything about chopping off heads.

"That's not true," said Peter.

"Yes it is," said Henry.

"Isn't!"

Horrid Henry sighed. "If you get it wrong, you'll be locked up in the Tower," he said. "It's high treason to greet the Queen the wrong way. *Everyone* knows that."

Perfect Peter paused. Mrs Oddbod hadn't said anything about being locked up in the Tower.

"I don't believe you, Henry," said Peter.

Henry shrugged.

"Okay. Just don't blame me when you get your head chopped off."

Come to think of it, thought Peter, there *was* a lot of head-chopping when people met kings and queens. But surely that was just in the olden days …

"MUM!" screamed Peter.

Mum ran into the room.

"Henry said I had to curtsey to the Queen," wailed Peter. "And that I'd get my head chopped off if I got it wrong."

Mum glared at Henry.

"How *could* you be so horrid, Henry?" said Mum. "Go to your room!"

"Fine!" screeched Horrid Henry.

"I'll practise with you, Peter," said Mum.

"Bow, bouquet, answer her question, walk away," said Peter, beaming.

The great day arrived. The entire school lined up in the playground, waiting for the Queen. Perfect Peter, dressed in his best party clothes, stood with Mrs Oddbod by the gate.

A large black car pulled up in front of the school.

"There she is!" shrieked the children.

Horrid Henry was furious. Miss Battle-Axe had made him stand in the very last row, as far away from the Queen as he could be. How on earth could he find out if she had 300 TVs standing way back here? Anyone would think Miss Battle-Axe wanted to keep him away from the Queen on purpose, thought Henry, scowling.

Perfect Peter waited, clutching an enormous bouquet of flowers. His big moment was here.

"Bow, bouquet, answer her question, walk away. Bow, bouquet, answer her question, walk away," mumbled Peter.

"Don't worry, Peter, you'll be perfect," whispered Mrs Oddbod, urging him forward.

Horrid Henry pushed and shoved to get
a closer view. Yes, there was his stupid
brother, looking like a worm.

Perfect Peter walked slowly towards the
Queen.

"Bow, bouquet, answer her question,
walk away," he mumbled. Suddenly that
didn't sound right.

Was it bow, bouquet? Or bouquet, bow?

The Queen looked down at Peter.

Peter looked up at the Queen.

"Your Majesty," he said.

Now what was he supposed to do next?

Peter's heart began to pound. His mind
was blank.

Peter bowed. The bouquet smacked him in the face.

"Oww!" yelped Peter.

What had he practised? Ah yes, now he remembered!

Peter curtseyed. Then he cocked a snook.

Mrs Oddbod gasped.

Oh no, what had he done wrong?

Aaarrgh, the bouquet! It was still in his hand.

Quickly Peter thrust it at the Queen.

Smack!

The flowers hit her in the face.

"How lovely," said the Queen.

"Waaaa!" wailed Peter. "Don't chop off my head!"

There was a very long silence. Henry saw his chance.

"How many TVs have you got?" shouted Horrid Henry.

The Queen did not seem to have heard.

"Come along everyone, to the display of Tudor daub-making," said Mrs Oddbod. She looked a little pale.

"I said," shouted Henry, "how many—"
A long, bony arm yanked him away.

"Be quiet, Henry," hissed Miss Battle-Axe. "Go to the back playground like we

practised. I don't want to
hear another word
out of you."

Horrid Henry
trudged off to the
vat of daub with
Miss Battle-Axe's
beady eyes
watching his every step. It was so unfair!

When everyone was in their assigned
place, Mrs Oddbod spoke. "Your Majesty,
mums and dads, boys and girls, the Tudors
used mud and straw to make daub for their
walls. Miss Battle-Axe's class will now
show you how." She nodded to the
children standing in the vat. The school
recorder band played *Greensleeves*.

Henry's class began to stomp in the vat
of mud and straw.

"How lovely," said the Queen.

Horrid Henry stomped where he'd been
placed between Jazzy Jim and Aerobic Al.

There was a whole vat of stomping
children blocking him from the Queen,
who was seated in the front row between
Miss Battle-Axe and Mrs Oddbod. If only
he could get closer to the Queen. Then he
could find out about those TVs!

Henry noticed a tiny space between
Brainy Brian and Gorgeous Gurinder.

Henry stomped his way through it.

"Hey!" said Brian.

"Oww!" said Gurinder. "That was my foot!"

Henry ignored them.

Stomp

Stomp

Stomp

Henry pounded past Greedy Graham and Weepy William.

"Oy!" said Graham. "Stop pushing."

"Waaaaaaa!" wept Weepy William.

Halfway to the front!

Henry pushed past Anxious Andrew and Clever Clare.

"Hellllppp!" squeaked Andrew, falling over.

"Watch out, Henry," snapped Clare.

Almost there! Just Moody Margaret and Jolly Josh stood in his way.

Margaret stomped.

Josh stomped.

Henry trampled through the daub till he stood right behind Margaret.

SQUISH. SQUASH. SQUISH. SQUASH.

"Stop stomping on my bit," hissed Moody Margaret.

"Stop stomping on *my* bit," said Horrid Henry.

"I was here first," said Margaret.

"No you weren't," said Henry. "Now get out of my way."

"Make me," said Moody Margaret.

Henry stomped harder.

SQUELCH! SQUELCH! SQUELCH!

Margaret stomped harder.

STOMP! STOMP! STOMP!

Rude Ralph pushed forward. So did Dizzy Dave.

STOMP! STOMP! STOMP!

Sour Susan pushed forward. So did Kung-Fu Kate.

STOMP! STOMP! STOMP! STOMP! STOMP!

A tidal wave of mud and straw flew

out of the vat.

SPLAT! Miss Battle-Axe was covered.

SPLAT! Mrs Oddbod was covered.

SPLAT! The Queen was covered.

"Oops," said Horrid Henry.

Mrs Oddbod fainted.

"How lovely," mumbled the Queen.

HORRID HENRY
TRICKS THE TOOTH FAIRY

(Originally published as
Horrid Henry and the Tooth Fairy)
Horrid Henry tries to trick the
Tooth Fairy into giving him more money,
sends Moody Margaret packing, causes his
teachers to run screaming
from school, and single-handedly
wrecks a wedding.

HORRID HENRY'S
NITS

Scratch. Scratch. Scratch. Horrid Henry
has nits – and he's on a mission to give
them to everyone else too. After that, he
can turn his attention to wrecking the
school trip, ruining his parents' dinner
party, and terrifying Perfect Peter.

HORRID HENRY BOOKS

Horrid Henry
Horrid Henry and the Secret Club
Horrid Henry Tricks the Tooth Fairy
Horrid Henry's Nits
Horrid Henry Gets Rich Quick
Horrid Henry's Haunted House
Horrid Henry and the Mummy's Curse
Horrid Henry's Revenge
Horrid Henry and the Bogey Babysitter
Horrid Henry's Stinkbomb
Horrid Henry's Underpants
Horrid Henry Meets the Queen
Horrid Henry and the Mega-Mean Time Machine
Horrid Henry and the Football Fiend
Horrid Henry's Christmas Cracker
Horrid Henry and the Abominable Snowman
Horrid Henry Robs the Bank

For younger readers
Don't Be Horrid, Henry!
Horrid Henry's Birthday Party